October 27TH

BY KEITH POOLE

KEITH POOLE

ISBN 978-0-578-10410-2

CONTENTS

This book is dedicated to
Marquel, Marquis and Amani Poole

Acknowledgements

I would like to acknowledge and thank Michael Ward of MDX Designs for the creation of my front and back book covers. To contact Michael Ward do so at www.michealdeangelodesigns.com.

I would also like to thank my sister in law Carla Huckleby-Poole for the hard work she did the editing my book thank you.

Thank you to all my family and friends who encouraged me during my writing process.

My name is Keith Poole I worked as a public transportation bus driver for a number of years. I have since retired from there and am now pursuing an active writing career. Writing short stories and poetry has always been a passion of mine. I am the proud father of three children whom I love with all my heart. They are my motivators and my inspiration in life. I am a strong believer in Jesus Christ in him all things are possible. The novel October 27th  is my entrance into the media world, I know you will enjoy it and look forward to more novels in the future. I would also like to thank my mother and father for all the love and encouragement without them there would be no me. I also would like to thank my brothers for all the love they gave. To my friend's thanks for all the good times and all the encouragement, I love you all from the bottom of my heart.

Chapter One

As the sunlight squeezed through the parted drapes welcoming in a new day, the distant echoing of the alarm crept into the sleep of the slumbering body of drunken flesh. Stank breath that once entered into a mind oblivious to time and space now entered into a tortured mind, one exploding in pain. As he reached over to cut off the blaring alarm, Jackson slid his chiseled muscular body from under the warmth of the covers, and sat on the edge of the bed cradling his pounding head with his huge hands.

"Damn is it time to get up already?" he grumbled.

"Shit! I can't stand waking up with a fucking hangover".

Disorientated by the effects of the alcohol, he could only think about the rundown feeling he was experiencing and rubbed his temples with his fingertips.

"Man my whole day is going to be fucked up".

He slowly rose to his feet on unsteady legs, "Oh well, time to face the music."

Struggling as he dragged his ass to the john, staggering and swaying all the way down the hall. Once there he put his hand on the wall behind the toilet to support himself.

After unzipping his trousers and pulling his dick out, he noticed there was bright red lipstick smeared from the head of his dick all the way down to his balls.

He began to pee but his aim was off to the left and he hit the wall beside the toilet. After getting his aim straight and finally peeing in the toilet, he finished his business and headed back toward the warmth and peacefulness of his bed.

Upon reaching it he lay on his back, and noticed a piece of paper folded in half sitting on the nightstand beside the bed. Jackson rolled over, retrieved the paper and opened it.

Still dizzy he had to close his eyes and refocus so he could read the letters. The paper turned out to be a check. Slowly he sat up and read it, all the while scratching his head in disbelief.

Pay to	Jackson Murphy
Amount of	Five hundred thousand dollars {500,000}
	Brenda Larson

Still staring at the check in his hand, he began to rub his neck and shoulders then his legs, because his body ached all over like someone had whooped his ass.

"Man what the fuck did I do last night?"

He tried to recall the evening's events in his mind, simultaneously letting out a sigh of foul smelling breath that crept into his nostrils.

"DAMN", he blurted out loud.

Slowly small images of last night's events began to sneak back into his mind. At first only very small excerpts, then like someone flipped on a light switch there it was live and in living color.

Chapter Two

Jackson remembered finishing working at the barbershop, and then Tyrone and some of his other homeboys were going to the state liquor store to cop some henny hen [for all you squares that's Hennessey].

"Let the games begin" shouted Jackson as he slid in to the passengers side of Tyrone's sleek ride, a light brown 1977 nine-eight with the candy paint.

Tyrone was Jackson's homeboy from way back. They liked to say they were brothers from another mother. Both liked to work out and were around 6'1 -6'2 and had basically the same muscular build.

The main difference was Jackson was caramel-colored and smooth with the ladies, and Tyrone was a dark chocolate version of him that tended to be shy, even though he was generally considered the better looking of the two men.

Tyrone started laughing while staring over at Jackson slowly pulling his pimp mobile into traffic he said, "Jackson you know we ain't got no cups for the drinks man." Jackson interrupted saying, "Don't worry about that. Let me do the thinking,"

"And you just do what you do best and drive," "You feel me?"

The drive to the state store was a short one, not really giving them time to talk. Jackson only thought about how the day had been thus far.

As they pulled into the parking lot of the liquor store, Jackson spotted a good parking spot. Pointing with his finger, he guided Tyrone as he pulled into the closest spot he could get to the front door. Joking and laughing they went into the state store.

"Are we going to cop the same old, same old?" asked Tyrone.

Looking over at the cashier Jackson smiled, gave a wink and said "You know it." The cashier, Mrs. Netty, was an older light-skinned lady that still could turn a head or two. She had worked as a cashier in the state store for several years, so she began to laugh as she grabbed the fifth of Hennessy and placed it in a brown paper bag. Jackson was a regular so she already knew what he meant by the same old, same old.

Reaching into his pocket, Jackson pulled out a new crisp fifty dollar bill and handed it to Mrs. Netty. As she was ringing up their purchase and handing Jackson his change, Jackson looked over at Tyrone, "Man, you can tighten me up later, you feel me?"

Tyrone looked back at Jackson, "You know I got you man."

Jackson gave Tyrone a look as to say yeah right. Since he was in the mood to party, now wasn't the time to worry about it. Waving goodbye and smiling, they exited the store and reached the car.

Tyrone looked over the roof of the car at Jackson, "You know what?"

Jackson looked back at him, "What now?"

"We forgot to get some cups for the drinks" Tyrone responded.

Jackson started to get frustrated. "Just open the door and let me in."

Tyrone opened his door and got in, and hit the power locks to unlock the passenger's side. Jackson got in and opened the brown paper sack the fifth of Hennessey was in.

Staring at Tyrone he grabbed the bottle by the neck and pulled out the cork,

"You soft ass nigga, only bitches need a cup, real soldiers drink right out the neck".

He took a swig.

"Sometimes you gotta let your nuts hang man".

He released his grip from the neck of the bottle, replaced the cork and put it back inside the brown paper sack. Slowly, he shook his head from side to side, "Tyrone man,"

"Sometimes I think if you weren't my homeboy, I'd swear you had some bitch in you. You feel me?"

With a look of anger and shock, Tyrone replied, "Man I don't feel shit you talking about.

"Why you always try and play me like I'm weak or something?"

"If I was really your homeboy, you wouldn't come at me like that." "Can you feel that?"

A pause then he smirked, "Plus I think you got some tendencies."

"What tendencies are you talking about", asked Jackson?

"You know what I'm talking about," Tyrone grinned as he backed out the parking spot.

"NO THE FUCK I DON`T!" Jackson yelled.

Tyrone raised one hand high into the air then with a slow descent back down, "Calm down brother."

"I was just joking with you man."

"You can give it, but you can't take it, can you?"

"Now who sounds like they got some bitch in them," he laughed uncontrollably.

Sneering back at his friend, Jackson could only muster up "Hee hee motherfucker that still doesn't change the fact that you got some bitch in you."

Sensing his anger and trying to ease the tension, Tyrone backed down.

"Man fuck all the jokes, it's time to get the party started."

Through his anger Jackson could see that Tyrone was trying to ease out of a confrontation, so he began to relax, "I heard that baby boy."

Chapter Three

Leaving the parking lot and pulling back into traffic, the light turned red. Sitting there waiting for the light to change, Tyrone casually checking his surroundings glanced over at the car to his left. He recognized the car beside them and with his fist over his mouth bellowed,

"Yo Jackson look at them markass niggas".

Jackson leaned forward trying to see who Tyrone was talking about started to chuckle.

"What's up hommie?"

Trouble leaned up to see Jackson on the passenger side, "Nothing chillin."

Tyrone peered into the back seat of the car to see if there was room for them to ride with them.

"What's up for tonight?"

"Like my name man, we're just out looking for some trouble".

The fact that he dressed like the grim reaper, always wearing black from head to toe, didn't help his cause. Trouble was the kind of guy that bad luck and misery loved. No matter where he was, or who he was with, something bad was bound to happen. You had to figure he was the most unlucky person on the face of the earth. So when he came around, people would say here comes Trouble. So the irony became reality.

Tyrone leaned over to whisper to Jackson, "Man let's ride with them,"

"It's only Trouble and Bullethead."

Now Bullethead's name came from the shape of his pointed head. The pointy top of his head and square jaws made it look like a bullet setting on his neck. When he was young everybody teased him about the shape of his head and would never respect the fact that his real name was Mark Jones. But after hearing every joke about him you could imagine, the name just kind of stuck to him. Plus it did look like an AK47 bullet on his neck walking around.

Trouble and Bullethead were known to always get shit started. But the mood that Jackson was in, he was like fuck it, whatever. I don't even care. I just want to have a good time.

Tyrone stared at Trouble," Why don't you and Bullethead follow us back over Jackson's house so we can drop my car off?"

"Then we can ride with yawl".

Leaning over to stop Tyrone and Jackson from hearing what he had to say, Trouble asked in a low whisper, "Bullethead what do you think?"

"Man do you want them riding with us all night?"

Bullethead responded, "Hell no."

"But I did see that bottle of henny they were trying to hide from us."

"Let's just ride them around until the bottle is gone."

"Then see ya, your ass is on your own," "You feel me?"

"Yep that's just what I was thinking my damn self." Trouble replied.

"Plus Jackson knows a lot of bitches, and we might luck up on something fucking with these lames".

"How much petro we got in the tank," asked Bullethead?

Trouble leaned up from his slumped position so he could read the gas gauge.

"Aw man, we got enough gas to ride them around until we drink up their shit. You feel me?"

"I feel you," laughed Bullethead.

Leaning back to his pimp daddy driving position, Trouble looked at Tyrone and said, "I think we can do that". He reached down to grab the remote controller to the radio from under the arm rest then turned the music up sky high. They gave each other dap and started cracking up, as they followed close behind Tyrone.

Tyrone, seeing in his rearview mirror, Trouble and Bullethead laughing, began to wonder how much of a good idea riding with them really was. Then the fact that he had just recently received another DUI hit home quickly.

In his mind he began to try and analyze and rationalize everything. He thought about Jackson telling him he wanted to drink and have a good time. So Tyrone knew he would be doing the driving tonight, and that made him feel a little uneasy.

He also remembered Jackson's statement in the state store.

Tyrone you can get me back later. In hood terms that meant I`ll buy the liquor and you do the driving. So passing the buck to someone else didn't seem that bad of an idea after all. He weighed out all the possibilities in his mind and figured the good outweighed the bad.

Plus he figured if Jackson didn`t object, then everything had to be cool. Jackson was Tyrone`s ace boon coon from way back. So if any bullshit was in the game he knew he was straight. Because I got his back, and I know he got mine.

Still feeling a little paranoid Tyrone felt down in the darkened car to where he kept his pea shooter, a little two shot Dillinger. It may be small, but it could fuck a nigga up; especially if you got real close. He thought about whether he should bring it with him, just in case, but then quickly decided against it. He knew it shouldn't come to that no matter what; because they were all old friends.

He remembered when they were all growing up together Jackson had already beaten up Trouble and Bullethead, so everything should be fine.

He still planned on keeping half way sober just to keep his eye on those cats. He thought about all the times Jackson and himself had kicked it and no matter who or what, Jackson always made sure everybody that was with him, always made it back home safe.

With that reassuring thought crossing his mind, he began to feel more like partying and less paranoid. Glancing over at Jackson, a friendly reassuring smile rolled across his lips.

Jackson was bobbing his head to the music coming from Trouble and Bullethead's car. Out of the corner of his eye, he caught a glimpse of the smile.

Turning quickly with a growl of a mean, junkyard dog, he yelled,

"MAN I AINT WITH THAT GAY SHIT!"

"I told you, I seen some bitch in you,"

"Tyrone you ever been tampered with?"

"Have you ever been to jail?"

Tyrone had been Jackson's best friend damn near his whole life; and Jackson knew whenever he teased him about being gay it really bothered him.

Jackson laughed until snot ran from his nose.

Wiping his nose he said, "Get back ain't cheating right."

Regaining his composure he stated seriously, "Let's have a bomb ass time tonight."

"We got to find some bitches and get some pussy, you feel me?"

Still very uncomfortable with Jackson's joke, Tyrone said,

"I heard that" and drove in an uneasy silence.

"Were you talking about all of us, or just about me and you with the bitches?"

Tyrone asked as he turned on Jackson's street.

Jackson looked at him, "Just because we're going to be riding with them, doesn't mean, I'm supplying the bitches for everybody. You feel me?"

He snorted, "If those cats ain't got enough game to get some pussy, then they are ass out."

"Or as the old saying goes, your SOL [Shit out of Luck]"

Tyrone gave Jackson a fist to fist pound, "I feel you man."

He pulled up in front of Jackson's house with Trouble and Bullethead almost bumper to bumper behind them.

Jackson got out of the car, looked back at the car close behind them and hollered to the men inside.

"I gotta run in and change real quick."

He suddenly realized they couldn't hear him because of the loud music, "Shit," he said. Walking alongside the driver's side of the car, he began to motion for Trouble to roll down the window so he could talk to him.

Trouble, seeing Jackson approach the car rolled the window half way down and stuck his ear up attentively.

"Turn down the fucking music man!" yelled Jackson.

The fact that he had to raise his voice started to give him an attitude.

Seeing the look of aggravation on Jackson's face, Trouble quickly turned down the music.

As his aggravation subsided, Jackson said, "Look here, since I'm already home I need to run inside and change my clothes."

"You know I just got off work and I want to freshen up a little,"

"So I can look good for the honnies tonight." "You feel me?"

"Man we weren't trying to be chillin over here all night" said Trouble.

"Man just give me about ten minutes to change my shit."

"I won't take long at all," "I'll be in and out real quick".

Jackson paused, "As a matter of fact, come in with us, that way I know you ain't trying to leave us."

Bullethead nudged Trouble and whispered, "Man I don't want to go in."

"They're going to fuck up our whole night."

Turning his body to hide his words from Jackson, Trouble whispered back "It's cool."

"Because we can go in," "Drink up all the henny, and then find some excuse to roll out on these lames. You feel me?"

Bullethead smiled and said, "That sounds damn good to me."

Trouble turned back to face the window, " We'll chill for a minute, and only a minute, you feel me?"

Jackson headed up his front steps and signaled to Tyrone to get out of the car and come on inside.

Tyrone thought to himself, should I leave the bottle of henny in the car? Or should I bring it in for these greedy motherfuckers to drink it all up? And then try to leave us on some bullshit ass excuse.

Then he figured it would probably be better to drink the henny in the safety of Jackson's house, then to be drinking and driving.

Another run in with the cops and he would do time for sure. Every time he thought about going to jail. He would think about the shit Jackson joked to him about. He had heard a lot of jail stories and some of them sounded real scary to him.

Plus if he did go to jail he knew Jackson would really pour on the gay jokes.

Chapter Four

Tyrone followed close behind Trouble and Bullethead up the front steps. Jackson turned the key in the door and then turned to them, "Don't be fucking up my place, you dig."

Trouble with a look of disgust said, "Man your pad ain't all that anyway. I don't know why you tripping." Tyrone laughed, "You must not have been over for a while, have you?" "This is a bonafide bachelor's pad."

Opening the door Jackson yelled," Welcome to the sugar-shack." Upon entering a silence fell on the two doubters.

"Man," said Trouble, almost drooling at the sight of Jackson's immaculate pad, "I didn't know you were chillin like this. I would have been done brought some bitches over here to chill with, you feel me?"

"Yall niggas need to take off your shoes" Jackson stated while removing his, "So you don't fuck up my carpet".

23

Once inside the all-white pristine carpet was the first thing to catch your eye. Then the butter soft white leather couch and matching love seat drew you in, practically begging you to sit and stay for a while.

The living room was accented with customized glass end tables with 24 carat gold legs, and a glass coffee table covered with Swarovski crystal figurines and there were plants everywhere. Orchids in almost every color and tropical plants dotted the room making it appear like a beautiful indoor garden.

Trouble had to ask, "What bitch decorated in here for you?" "Because I know you ain't got taste like this".

"Motherfucker", Jackson responded, "Just because you don't have class doesn't mean everybody else can't have some."

Passing his living room they all entered the family room, still nice but nothing like his show piece living room. There was some leather furniture and a few pictures that dotted the walls. But the main attraction was the entertainment pieces in the room, his stereo system and television.

Jackson asked Tyrone, "Did you grab the bottle out of the car?"

"Yeah I got it", he said grudgingly.

"Does anybody need any ice?" Jackson asked.

Tyrone spoke up first. "Hell yeah, this shit ain't no joke straight."

Jackson pointed toward the entry way, "Look here man, go around in the kitchen and grab four glasses and a bowl of ice, will you?"

"Yeah, sure man" said Tyrone and left the room

Jackson picked up a large remote, pushed one of the numerous buttons on it and pointed it at his 71 inch flat screen TV mounted on the wall. "Turn on the stereo while I change Bullethead."

"You don't mind if I touch your stereo?" Bullethead asked.

"Naw man" Jackson replied, "I just told you to turn it on. Just hit the power button and everything will come right on".

Bullethead pushed the power button. The sound of some mellow smooth jazz drifted into the air making everybody lean back and allow the music to take control. Jackson left the room.

"Who is that?" asked Trouble?

"I don't know, but that's a bad ass jam," said Tyrone re-entering the room. Giving everybody a glass and ice, he asked in general, "What's the plan for tonight?"

Pouring their drinks, Trouble said, "Like I told you earlier, we were just cruising around looking for something to get into" "We just happened to run into you and Jackson." In his mind he was thinking I'm glad we did, because now we get to drink for free, because my pockets are on empty, ha ha.

Bullethead spoke up, "I don't know about you and Jackson, but I'm looking for some ass tonight." "Let's go to the club and get some honnies to come back over here and chill tonight.

Tyrone spoke up, "Man I don't know" "You better ask Jackson first." "But I don't think he'll mind." As Jackson was heading up the step, Tyrone hollered out, "What do you think about doing some entertaining here tonight homeboy?"

Pausing at Tyrone`s comment, Jackson said, "Look here can I please get dressed first?"

"Then we can discuss whatever, you heard me?"

Jackson reached the top of the steps and began to think about the possibility of actually entertaining some females in his home. Then the past experiences of trying to entertain with other homeboys with some females came roaring back, specifically how their jealousy prevented the evening from being a success.

It was very disturbing that someone you call a friend would act so negatively to try to impress a female. He figured that if he was willing to share his home and supply all the refreshments, then a person invited to his home, which he considered his palace, would not act so fucked up.

But shit happens.

He knew no matter how nice and cool you try to be to someone, if they are screwed up mentally then all your efforts are in vain.

He began to remember one night at the club with Tyrone. At the club everything was fine. The drinks were flowing, the music was bumping, and the dance floor was packed, just a perfect party atmosphere.

Then suddenly the club was closing and no one wanted to go home.

Tyrone, with his eye on the pretty young lady he watched all night, walked over to her and touched her hand, "Excuse me, how about we go over to my friend's house and keep partying?"

The young lady looking at Tyrone asked, "What about my friend,"

"Do you have someone for her?"

"If not, then I can't go."

"We came together and we'll leave together."

Tyrone started to smile, "That's no problem."

"I think she'll love my friend right there," He pointed to Jackson showing her who he was talking about.

Tyrone figured as long as he was hooking Jackson up with her friend, then he shouldn't mind doing some entertaining.

Before he could react, Jackson was sucked in and committed to supplying his home and services.

Pulling Tyrone to the side by the bottom of his shirt he said, "Man, don't you ever volunteer anything that has to do with me ever again."

"We really don't know these bitches just to be inviting them back to my house like that, you feel me?"

Jackson looked to the dance floor, "Plus I really didn't feel like a house full of people."

"I had my mind set on chillin, and have a close intimate one on one, with that honey over there." He pointed to the woman he had danced with all night, "You feel me?"

The skin tight second skin she wore as a dress made her irresistible. Her body just called to Jackson for some personal attention. Every time they touched as they danced was a reiteration of the sexual attraction they both felt between them.

Jackson had been putting in work with her all night. He knew that once he asked her to come home with him it was on, but still being pressured by Tyrone, he gave in. He walked over to the young lady he had primed for that night to ask her for her number. Tapping her on her shoulder he said, "Excuse me, I would like to get to know you and possibly see you again."

"Can we exchange numbers to keep in contact?"

The young lady hearing Jackson ask for her number looked disappointed. She had already made her mind up she was going to go home with him.

Not wanting to loose contact with him she reached into her purse and retrieved a pen and paper to write down her number.

After writing down her number and handing it to him she whispered,

"I would have gone home with you; I was just waiting for you to ask."

Starting to walk away she said, "Call me" and faded into the night with everyone else still lingering around the club.

After Jackson heard those words he got upset; then almost instantly the fact that he had her made him relax. He knew after a good conversation she would still be ready.

Walking back to where Tyrone waited for him he said, "If you wanted to volunteer a place to go and still party, then you should have volunteered your pad."

With a look of disappointment Tyrone said, "You know I would have, but we wouldn't have had much fun in my one bedroom efficiency," "Where we all going to sit?"

"You know I only have that small beat up blue couch."

"How about the entertainment,"

"You want me to play my clock radio?"

"We would have been the laughingstocks at the club next week."

He pulled his jacket closed, "These bitches would have got right on the phone and called everybody they could think of,"

"You know a rumor only takes two people saying the same thing,"

"Too two different people, and then it's a chain-reaction, you feel me?"

Tyrone rubbed his hands, getting more upset by the minute, "These bitches would have said how small my pad was and called us cheap."

"I can just hear them now saying how we call ourselves pimps, and players, and ain't got shit." He paused, "Jackson man, they would have told every female they knew that these two guys ain't shit."

"I can imagine walking into the club next week, and these same honeys might be sitting at the bar, and as soon as they see us start to laugh and point us out."

"Saying shit like these two players, or excuse me want to be players, tried to holler last week."

"They had the nerve to try to take us to some dump, where we couldn't even sit down."

"I thought a player would have it going on."

Jackson picturing all that Tyrone had talked about felt trapped because his statement started to make good sense to him. But the fact that he was being pressured into being hospitable made him upset.

Tyrone continued talking, mimicking a woman's voice, "These want to be players are perpetrators."

"Yeah they look good and dress good, but it's just an illusion."

"Fucking around with these two you'll be sorely disappointed."

"These guys are a couple of lames."

Jackson knew a lot of women, and it wouldn't take long for a rumor to spread about him, because of his popularity. And his reputation was very important to him.

He always felt like he was a player and players represent.

Meaning if you got it, then flaunt it, that way it's not bragging if you're just doing what you do, you feel me? Some people just talk about what they have, and in reality don't have anything.

Then some people have it all, but don't look good having it.

For example, picture a candy red S600 Mercedes convertible with the top down and a seventy-five year old, wrinkled woman, driving twenty miles per hour down a busy street. She wouldn't look too appealing to most guys.

Now take that same car and put in a twenty-five year old, caramel colored woman built like a brick house, and watch heads turn as she drives by.

People wouldn't say she was bragging, because she looked good in that car, she was flaunting what she had, and looked good doing it ,you feel me?

Jackson felt like he had established himself in the streets, and when he was around people took notice. He always said, some people talk about it, and some people will be about it.

Through all his hard work, sweat, and toil, he had made a pretty good living for himself. He had a nice car, fine clothes; excuse me I mean shit sharp clothes.

He had just recently purchased a couple of rental properties to add to his player status. To be a player in his eyes you had to have shit that any old lame couldn't get. People would have to admire you as a man and how you carried yourself.

Besides all of that you had to be a ladies man. You had to have what it takes to attract the finest women around. The ones the average Joe normally would be afraid to approach.

If you feel like you got what it takes, then flaunt it, and if you can flaunt it, and look good doing it, then it ain't bragging, you feel me? You're just representing being a player.

Chapter Five

Tyrone hollered up from the bottom of the steps, "Hey player what's taking you so long?"

"Only bitches take that long to get dressed."

"What are you doing, playing with yourself?"

Tyrone began to laugh from the stupidity the alcohol was making him feel.

Hearing the comment Tyrone made about Jackson, Trouble jumped in.

"Taking that long to get dressed, he'll be prettier than the bitches," as he poured another drink.

"If we don't get any pussy tonight, we can fuck him."

"You feel me Bullethead?"

"As long as I can go first," stated Bullethead sloshing down a drink and pouring another one.

The effect of the henny had taken over their rational thinking. Jackson thought about the comments being made as he approached his closet said, "A drunk ain't shit."

"I wonder if I sound that ignorant when I'm buzzed off henny."

Then he shook his head, "Naw, I got too much game to be like them cats down stairs."

"A true player always holds his composure."

"Through thick and thin, right times and tight times, you'd better represent."

"And that's why I'm a player."

Opening the door to his walk-in closet, he tried to decide what look he was trying to achieve tonight. Go to the club dapper or go casual?

He had to consider who he was riding with; if he got too clean it would give the rest of the guys he was with an attitude.

So he had to think about them in determining what outfit he was going to wear for the evening.

Then he said out loud, not even realizing he was even doing it.

"Fuck them; I'm going to go to the club the way I always go."

That was to be one of the freshest dressed people, if not the freshest dressed person in the club.

That included males as well as females. Even the honeys would admire the way he dressed. They would always give him compliments on his style of dress.

His style of dress, in his mind was based on your mind set. If you thought good of yourself, then you should look good. The two went together like a hand and a glove.

A player should not only look the part, you had to live the part. Women can recognize the real from the fake. A player shouldn't have to explain himself; his appearance should speak for itself.

Roaming through the closet he thought about the different outfits he had worn to the club previously. To impress the honeys you never repeated an outfit twice within at least six months to a year time frame.

That way the first impression you would make would be a lasting one. And the anticipation for your next arrival would be even more spectacular.

Strolling through his suits a tag peaked out from the middle of the rest of the outfits. Separating the clothes he noticed it was something he had forgotten about. It was wedged in between two suit jackets barely exposed it was a canary yellow velvet silk suit.

Now to the average Joe or lame the colors might sound crazy.

But given to a player; woo-wee. A player would show his ass, and look good doing it .I mean extremely good. Along with the velvety silk suit, there was a pair of matching yellow and white gators [alligator-shoes].

"Pimping ain't easy but somebody has to do it."

He poked his chest out and raised his head feeling himself as an air of confidence swooped onto him some people might not understand.

But his fascination with clothes; and always aiming to be the best at whatever he did made him feel good.

Maybe it was the thought of how the velvety material would feel on his body and flow freely as he strolled into the club.

Making all the honnies break their necks to look at him and smile as he passed by. Jackson smiled while holding the suit up to his match the shirt and tie together.

If you were on the outside looking in you might say I'm conceited. But you have to understand where I come from, a young and poor black male from the ghetto trying to get it how he lived.

The typical person from the suburbs won't understand that statement. The statement get it how you live refers to making the best out of the resources available to you.

Which usually when you're from the hood or ghetto, it's slim to none.

So to see me with all this confidence you have to wonder; do I think I'm better than everybody else. Growing up in the projects, most poor people desperately trying to survive day by day have low self-esteem, but not me.

All my life I wondered if there was more to life than what I saw every day, all the misery and violence in the hood.

It was disheartening for me to see how hard life was for some people. But then I realized only the strong survive.

At an early age I decided to be one of the strongest around. I decided if I had to be in the ghetto, I'd be the best the ghetto had ever seen.

Armed with the street smarts of a grown man, as my mama used to say, I worked my hand at an early age or whenever given a chance.

Most grown folks around me were impressed how mature I was, even in my conversation. I was already establishing myself among known players.

I would watch their walks and noticed they didn't just walk like everybody else, but each player had his own signature walk, almost like a brand. They would stroll with a confidence that was cocky and almost vain.

I would listen to their conversations and see how smooth they approached women and not only the women from the ghetto, but also ones from the suburbs. Back in the day there was an invisible line you just didn't cross.

You would think most of these women would not have a conversation, let alone the time of day for these types of guys. But the game they spit was so strong it made the women melt in their hands.

Seeing all this at an early age showed me, that if you didn't believe in yourself, get off your ass and make whatever it is in life you wanted to happen; happen, then nine times out of ten it won't happen.

Some of the older men around the hood would always make little comments that back then I really didn't understand until I got a little older. Like don't put off tomorrow what you can do today.

As a kid I thought there's always a tomorrow. But as you grow older life teaches you that tomorrow is not promised to anyone.

One by one all the guys I watched growing up began to pass away, leaving room for the next generation of players to follow suit. But in my mind, I always thought the old players had strong game.

Times have changed, so the game has to be improved. Terminology has changed. I knew a player couldn't approach a woman these days and say, "Say mama what's happening?"

How's about we slide to my hog and dip around the corner to the bar?"

Back then that was a strong line. It showed your hand. First of all it showed you had some ends to spend [money].

It also showed you were riding right. If you had a hog {a Cadillac}, then you definitely were handling your business. You know, to ride in a hog you had to dress to impress. Clean from head to toe, all day, every day, you feel me?

The old players or OG`s followed and respected the rules to the game. O yeah there are rules to the game; and if you don't know about them then consider yourself a lame.

The streets are governed by specific rules that are never talked about or written down. But when you grow up in the streets, you learn and understand them quite clearly.

To be considered a player, people have to respect your game. Whether a hustler, a pimp, or a player.

A square might think all three are the same thing. But they're all different, but tie into one another. A hustler will sell any product to make money i.e. [drugs, pills, clothes, jewelry, cars]; anything to make a buck.

Now a pimp's main source of income is strictly bitches, no more no less. Now a player, my expertise, I gets it how I live baby. A player has some hustling skills; a certain degree of pimping skills, and a mouth piece that just won't quit.

A player's main skill is his conversation. Being able to talk your way into anything you want or need. A player must have class. There will always be an overwhelming amount of confidence oozing from every pore of 1 of his body.

A player's style of dress will set him apart from all others, that particular flavor only a player can represent.

People give players props over pimps, because there is no violence to the game. Players also receive props over hustlers because there is no stealing involved. Strictly using his game, a player can get a woman to do what a pimp can't; without whooping her ass.

A player can also use his hustling skills to survive without being deceitful. That's what I admired the most growing up. I respected the fact that the players I saw growing up were also gentlemen. They were smart, had class, and brought respect to the game.

Now that I'm representing, I carry the burden of elevating the game to a higher level. Always remembering the past and giving respect to the old players. And taking all I learned and applying it to the game, while taking the game to the next level.

Chapter Six

As Jackson strolled down memory lane, he lost track of time and forgot his main purpose for going upstairs.

Then a loud voice called to him," Jackson, what the fuck you doing up there?"

"Get dressed and come on down so we can go."

"I'm ready to go to the club and see some bitches, you feel me," yelled Tyrone. Tyrone was buzzing real good from the Hennessy and now knew he wanted the responsibility of driving left up to someone else.

Seeing the bottle of henny slowly begin to disappear, Trouble asked, "What time is it any way?" "I know it's getting late."

Bullethead spoke up, "I told you they were going to fuck up our night."

Trouble looking at Tyrone to see his reaction to Bulletheads statement, says "Shut up Bullethead you talk too much.' 'Tyrone man, please excuse my partner, he's had too much to drink." He gave a cheesy smile, "Why don't you go up stairs to see how long Jackson is going to be?"

With an attitude Tyrone responded "Yeah sure."

As soon as Tyrone left the room Trouble whispered to Bullethead, "Why you running off at the mouth?"

"Man." Bullethead tried to answer to his defense, but Trouble didn't give him a chance to respond.

"Shut up," "I don't want to hear it you almost got us into some shit."

"You know how sensitive Jackson can be," he shook the bottle, "I really don't feel like getting into it with him now that I'm drunk, you feel me?"

"Well how about we just dip out on them like we had planned from the beginning, while they're upstairs."

Trouble thought about Bulletheads comment for a second, "We'll just say you got sick from drinking too much; and we had to leave because we didn't want to fuck up Jackson's bathroom."

Starting to smile Bullethead stood up, "That sounds cool to me, let's go." They slowly crept to the front door and made their getaway undetected.

Approaching Jackson's bedroom, Tyrone could hear the shower running and hollered,

"Yo Jackson hurry up, Trouble and Bullethead are trying to leave us."

Jackson could only hear a small part of what Tyrone was trying to tell him, because of the low roar of the water. Yelling in a loud voice Jackson said, "I'll be out in a hot second."

Turning off the water, he wrapped a towel around himself and exited the bathroom. Looking at Tyrone's face he could see the effects of the alcohol all over him, "Now what were you saying when I was in the shower?"

Tyrone started to speak but began to slur.

"I was t-t-trrying to tell you,"

He paused to try to speak better.

"Trouble and Bullethead are trying to leave us."

"They drank up almost the whole bottle, but I made them save you a swallow".

"Thanks man I appreciate that," said Jackson.

"Go and tell them I'll be ready in ten minutes."

In the distance Tyrone could hear Trouble's music pound out the beats, as he headed down the stairs. He stopped in his tracks and dropped his head, "Damn, they did just what I was thinking about earlier."

"Jackson is going to be pissed off."

He knew then the idea of having a good night was out of the question, and turned and took his time heading back up the steps dreading telling Jackson the bad news.

Entering the bedroom again Tyrone said in a slow drawn out fashion, "Yo Jackson, those niggas snuck out on us man."

"When I got downstairs I could hear their music down the block."

He stood against the wall, "So now I guess the night is over."

A smile began to form on Jackson's face. With a puzzled look Tyrone asked, "What are you smiling about?"

"I just told you they left us and all you can do is smile, is something wrong with you?"

With a look of confusion Tyrone asked, "You alright?"

Jackson had dried off and put on his robe.

"Tyrone man, I'm cooler than a fan."

" I'm glad they left."

"Now we can really party. You feel me?"

"Once I found what I wanted to wear I knew those cats might start to hate on us tonight, and might have fucked up our pussy for the evening."

"So you telling me they left us, that's good news to me."

Tyrone interrupted, "So how are we going to get to the club Mr. Smiley pants?"

"I know I owe you, but I ain`t trying to drive, you feel me?"

"Not after almost a whole fifth to the head".

Laughing at Tyrone's question Jackson said, "Seriously have you forgotten who I am?" "When I want it to happen, baby boy, I can make it happen"

"Throw me my black book over on the night stand will you?"

Tyrone grabbed the black book and tossed it to Jackson.

"What kind of mood are you in Tyrone?"

"You want something wild, something laid back, or just a stone cold freak?"

Beginning to smile, Tyrone folded his arms and stared into the air pondering what Jackson had just presented to him; and thought about it before answering.

"Hmm let me see."

"I'm in the mood for a freak, because a freak will never say no."

Jackson opened the book and let his finger scroll down through the numbers.

"Cool, I think I can handle that".

Stopping at a name followed by several stars, he smiled.

"My man, I think you're in luck."

In his mind he began to picture the young lady whose number he had stopped at, and recalled her beautiful smile. The fact that she was built like a brick house didn't hurt. She had long muscular legs that led up to a bodacious, firm ass that you could sit a drink on. In the hood we say baby got back, you feel me? She was also the most beautiful, young thing around.

Chapter Seven

He had met Tamika around a year ago when she came into the barber shop with her brother Big R. He wanted a haircut on his birthday and had already received one of Jackson's cards. One of his best friends had just come from the shop. Having gotten his hair cut the week earlier, he was bragging how good the barber was.

So Big R decided he would check Jackson out. Big R was a six-foot-six ex basketball star turned local neighborhood hustler. When his dreams of becoming a part of the NBA fizzled he turned to the streets instead of pursuing his education.

His parents were very disappointed, but he vowed not to be a statistic and to always care for his younger sister, because he wanted her to get the education he had rejected when he had the opportunity.

Tamika and Big R walked into an empty shop except for Jackson. Motioning to Big R Jackson said, "You're next" and pointed to the chair.

"How do you want it man?"

Big R sat down, "Even all over with a n with a nice line up".

While Jackson was cutting his hair, he happened to mention how lucky Big R was to have such a beautiful lady, referring to the young lady sitting in the waiting area reading a magazine.

He responded, "Aw man, that's just my sister."

"As a matter of fact, you should holler at her because she's single."

Jackson interrupted to greet some more people as they came into the shop. Big R finishing his statement said, "She was fucking around with some old cornball ass dude." He laughed, "But since he was a lame I had to put an end to that, you feel me?"

Jackson replied with a smile, "I feel you man."

"A woman that fine deserves someone to treat her special," and in his mind he was referring to himself.

Tamika was light-skinned with green eyes and had long beautiful silky black hair that accented her delicate features. He looked over at Big R's sister, "Excuse me can you come over here for a second please?"

The young lady sitting there waiting for her brother looked around to see who Jackson was speaking to. While looking from side to side, pointing her finger at herself she asked,

"Are you talking to me?"

"Yes," said Jackson, smile still in place.

She approached him, "I don't know you do I?"

"No not yet But I would like to introduce myself."

"My name is Jackson, Jackson Murphy, and what is your name sweet thing?" He extended his hand.

"My name is not sweet thing it's Tamika" she stated in an irritated voice, pulling her Fendi bag onto her shoulder.

She shook Jackson's hand, "How are you doing?"

"I'm doing just fine now, because you made my day."

"The only thing I need to happen now is to win a million bucks."

"Because that's the only thing that can top the fact that I just met the most beautiful young lady I've ever seen in my life."

Her brother still sitting in the chair began to laugh.

"Damn man you sure are smooth".

Jackson continued to stare, "Naw, I aint trying to be smooth, just speaking the truth."

"Tamika, do you mind if I ask you a personal question?"

"Go ahead", she said, staring right back at him.

Pausing before he took off the chair cloth from around his client, Jackson already knew the answer to the question, "Do you have a man in your life?"

Tamika began to answer, her face a little sad as she tried not to show the pain of her most recent break up, "No I don't."

Jackson responded, "That's wonderful, because I would love for us to get to know one another."

I'll give you my number, and when you have a chance, give me a call."

"Maybe we can go out to dinner, or to a movie." "Better yet, I would love to just hold your hand, and go for a walk in the park."

Not even realizing it, a huge smile formed on her face. "Are you just saying that to me, or do you say that to all the women you meet?" she asked fiddling with the half carat diamond earring on her left ear.

Jackson exposing his swagger responded, "No I don't. I only do special things for special people."

"I think you're special. Like a rare flower that needs to be cared for."

"Baby I just want to make you smile, because it seems to me it's been a while since you smiled."

"So whatever I have to do to make you smile, I'm willing to do it".

Turning his back to Tamika he said. "Hold on, while I write down the number for you."

He wrote down his number, handed it to Tamika slowly and softly caressed her hand while staring deep into her eyes. Tamika instantly felt quivers run up her arm from his touch. The slow caress from Jackson started to arouse her.

Smiling while staring down at the number she made a mental note to find out more about Jackson, because she already knew she wanted him.

Turning away from Tamika to face his client with his hand already extended Jackson said,

"By the way my name is Jackson Murphy."

"Come back and see me again."

Looking in the mirror and admiring Jackson's handy work, Big R began to smile. Shaking Jackson`s hand he responded, "By the way my name is Robert, but they call me Big R." Still admiring the hair cut and smiling he stated, "I'll be back next week."

"Cool" said Jackson, "Call me to set up the appointment." He handed Big R his card, "Here's my card with the number to the shop".

"Alright Jackson, I'll call you next week for sure," said Big R.

As Tamika and Robert turned to leave the barbershop Jackson could only stare in amazement. Her ass looked like two whole hams, swinging from side to side inside her skin tight dress.

Slowly, Tamika turned to wave goodbye to Jackson and a smile formed on her face, because as she suspected he was staring at her ass. Jackson already knew the physical attraction was there, he just wondered how her mind was.

Entering the car, Tamika turned to her brother "So what do you think about Jackson?"

"Who," he asked while starting the car?

She rolled her eyes, "The barber that just cut your hair".

"Oh him, he was cool I guess," said Big R.

"Why are you asking?"

"I'm just curious about your opinion of him", she said.

"From what I can see he seems alright, I guess."

"Do you plan on getting to know him?" he asked.

"Maybe," said Tamika, "I'll have to spend some time with him, but I think I like him."

"I want to see if he's full of games, or if he's all he portrays to be."

Driving away, Tamika started to wonder about forming a friendship with Jackson. She often would meet someone and allow her mind to get carried away in what could be. She never gave herself a chance to know the person after the first introduction.

Not really knowing what she was getting herself into, she would dive head first into a new relationship. She often went on the first impression, which in most cases is not always the truth.

Most people put their best foot forward when they first meet someone, and this may not be who they really are.

Her bad decisions always led to her getting her feelings hurt. She would call her girlfriends, telling them she had met the perfect guy. How charming he was, or how cute he was.

But in the end it was her youth that made her susceptible to game. She was too naive when it came to being able to read someone, or being able to deal with relationships.

Staring at the number he had stopped at, he began to recall their first date. Tamika had called him the next day inviting him to have a drink after work. She asked if she could pick him up from work.

"Sure," said Jackson "I'll be off at six o `clock."

"I'll be there to pick you up at six", she said. After a hard day of work, Jackson was looking forward to spending a little time to relax and unwind. Tamika pulled up as he was getting off.

"I'm glad you were on time," said Jackson.

"To be honest with you, I've been thinking about you every since we met."

"I was looking forward to seeing you too," said Tamika. She drove to a nice upscale tavern she sometimes visited. She was trying to show Jackson she was not some hood rat with a big ass and a pretty smile. She wanted to show him she had some class.

At the tavern, while eating and drinking, they talked about their perspective hopes and dreams.

From their conversation alone, Tamika was really falling for Jackson. As the date was coming to an end, she decided she wanted to sleep with him. He had been the perfect gentleman and made her feel special all night. Also, like her he had plans for a better future. She could see this going long-term and didn't want to wait too long to get things started.

Jackson in his mind was thinking how good the date had been, "So when can I see you again?"

Tamika responded, "I was hoping you would invite me over to your place tonight."

Beginning to smile, but not really considering sleeping with her, Jackson said "Sure why not."

She took Jackson to pick up his car at the barber shop, and followed him to his home. Upon entering, she was impressed how Jackson's house was decorated.

Jackson said, "Have a seat."

"Would you like something to eat, or drink," he asked.

"No I'm fine," said Tamika.

Jackson dimmed the lights and put on some slow jams to set the mood, then slid down beside Tamika and stared into her eyes.

He began to caress her hand while gently kissing her neck. The slow jams, the dimmed lights, along with the softness of his touch were having an effect on Tamika.

Starting to get hot she asked, "Do you mind if I get comfortable?"

"No," said Jackson.

The drinks at the tavern had already taken affect and she was ready for what the night would bring. She stood up and released the two straps supporting her dress. It slowly slid down revealing her beautiful naked body. For a second, the shock of her undressing took Jackson's breath away.

At the same time, seeing her beautiful naked body standing there accented by the dim lights, made Jackson's dick hard. "Do you like what you see", she asked, running her hands up and down her body.

"I would be crazy not to," he said.

"Baby, you have one of the most beautiful bodies I've ever seen in my life."

Her breasts were the perfect size, more than enough to fill his hands,(and Jackson had big hands). Large protruding nipples, the size of the top part of your baby finger, made his mouth water. His eyes slowly slid down her body admiring every inch of her beauty.

He was amazed how perfect she was a man would have to be a fool not to want her.

As she leaned forward her perky breasts were just inches from Jackson's awaiting mouth. The thought of sucking them made the anticipation even more unbearable.

She pulled him to his feet and began to undress him.

After they were naked, she kissed his nipples softly and caressed his butt. In his mind, Jackson thought how Tamika was treating him like he was the woman. But he quickly decided to go along with it.

She kissed and licked her way down his body, aiming straight for his manhood.

A big smile lit up her face. "What do we have here," she exclaimed in delight and fell to her knees.

Looking up, she stared into Jackson's eyes as she began to suck his dick, slowly swallowing his massive tool inch by inch. Her mouth was full and strained to hold him in. Reaching down he eased her mouth from around him, then grabbed her by the arms. He pulled her to her feet, and turned her to face the back of the couch, so he could hit it from the rear.

Everything else could come later, but he had to have her now. Understanding what he wanted, she quickly spread her legs, exposing her hot and wet pussy. Tamika couldn't wait to feel him inside of her.

Nothing was better than a big dick rammed inside a tight pussy, doing its thing, creating its magic. That's if the owner knew how to use it right.

In the past she often spent months getting to know someone, only to discover he was a dud in the bedroom. For her a dud was a little dick or a big dick but no skills.

Jackson bent over her and parted her pink pussy lips with the head of his cock, pushing it in and going slow to give her time to adjust to his size. Though not as large as Jackson, she was used to boyfriends with big dicks. These days she wouldn't settle for less.

Halfway in he began to thrust in and out, with his hands on both sides of her hips. His big body dwarfed her smaller frame. Tamika rocked her ass back to meet his thrusts, content to let him take the lead.

"Harder…more" she panted' her long hair moving back and forth with her frantic movements.

She was squeezing her inner lips as he moved into her and the friction almost made him come. He slowed down before he embarrassed himself by getting his rocks off and leaving her hanging.

If it was one thing he prided himself on, it was his lovemaking skills. No woman he had been with could complain about him leaving her unsatisfied. He knew how to use his dick, which was another reason the ladies flocked to him. Women talked and word got around; and eventually they wanted to test it for themselves. He moved deeper inside of her until their hairs were entwined. He could feel the juices seeping from her hole, like someone was pouring hot liquid down his legs.

"Baby girl, you are so tight", he gasped, "I want to stay here forever, live in this sweet pussy".

"Harder Jackson," she moaned, twisting her head from to side to side, "Fuck me harder".

He went back to pounding her pussy fast and hard just as she wanted.

Tamika felt like she was in heaven. Jackson's thick dick was making her insides quake. Her legs felt so weak. Every time he pulled out and pushed back in he hit her clit, and caused sensations she had never felt before. None of her past boyfriends had fucked her this good.

Jackson moved both hands to her pussy and rubbed her clit.

"Oh, oh!" she whimpered. Then he gathered some of her juices on his right fingers and moved them behind her. He loved plump beautiful asses and had noticed hers from the start. He rubbed her juices in her asshole and then stuck one finger in as deep as he could. He then added a second finger and started rotating them.

Feeling the pressure of one finger on her clit, his other fingers deep in her ass, and the continuous pounding of his dick, she started to convulse uncontrollably. She came with a loud scream and her world exploded in ecstasy.

Her body jerked violently and tried push his dick out of her, but it was too long and deeply buried in her. Feeling her orgasm he removed his fingers from her ass. With a vise like grip around her hips, he eased his dick out of her and then forcibly slammed it back in. Doing this repeatedly and trying to make her cum again.

She was limp and hanging over the back of the couch with Jackson supporting most of her weight. After a few minutes of this she stiffened and came again, and the sound of her moans and the softness of her body took Jackson over the edge.

He took his dick, soaked with her juices, from inside her pussy and pushed her to the floor. Standing over her, he shot his hot load and showered her naked body. He loved seeing women covered in his cum. It was the next best thing besides watching them swallow it.

With a huge smile on his face he collapsed next to her and gazed into her eyes.

"Baby, you wore me out."

"That pussy is out of this world".

He put his arm around her and they both drifted off into a deep sleep.

Tyrone asked, "So why did you stop seeing her?"

With a look of disappointment he said, "Because she ended up being a big freak."

"I should have realized it when I slept with her on the first date."

"But that's not unusual for me, so I didn't see it coming." He closed the book.

"That's all she wanted to do, was fuck all day, every day."

"She just couldn't hold my interest."

"But it's alright." "We had fun together while it lasted."

"I'll give her a call in a minute so you can speak to her."

"Tyrone hand me the phone will you," said Jackson.

Tyrone handed Jackson the phone, and Jackson began to dial the number. The phone rang a few times, and then the low seductive voice of the goddess on the other end came drifting into his ear. "Hello," answered Tamika.

"Hey baby," said Jackson.

"Whose calling?" asked Tamika.

"This is Jackson. Are you busy?" he asked.

"No," responded Tamika eagerly.

He could hear a note of excitement in her voice. "Baby I would love to see you tonight."

"Do you think it's possible we could get together to have a drink with some friends? ".

"Sure", said Tamika, "You already know I'll do anything you ask me to do,"

"And I do mean anything,"

"That's cool baby, because I have a surprise for you" Jackson said,

"I think you'll like it a lot, , what time will you be ready?"

"I can be ready in about an hour," said Tamika.

"Cool baby that sounds good give me a call when you're heading this way." Tamika began to smile. Jackson asked, "Tamika would you please put on something sexy for me?"

"How sexy do you want me? Do you want easy access or just pretty," she asked.

"I'll leave that up to you to decide because I already know which ever you choose; you're going to look good."

Tamika began to smile on the other end of the line. She liked that fact that Jackson trusted her judgment.

"Call me when you're on the way, bye baby", said Jackson.

"Bye baby" she said in a deep sexy moan.

Hanging up the phone, Jackson told Tyrone, "It's on baby."

"Solid," said Tyrone. "Do you mind if I find something to wear out of your closet?" Looking at Jackson's face he tried to judge his response. He was uneasy asking him the question, because he knew Jackson valued his clothes.

Jackson looked hard at Tyrone for asking that type of question responded,

"Now you already know how I am about my clothes."

"You know I normally don't let people borrow anything, but since you're my homeboy and all," he slapped Tyrone on the back, "And I want you to make a good impression on this little honnie,"

"I'll make an exception for you." "You feel me?"

"Cool, man, you know I appreciate this."

"No problem, Tyrone. Just don't make it a habit, and don't pick something people have already seen me in," "Because you'll get the wrong response."

"As a matter of fact, I should have a matching blue velvety silk suit in the closet that I've never wore."

"Why don't you look in there and see if you can fit it."

"What about the shoes," asked Tyrone?

Jackson began to smile, "Man you sure are pushing it."

"Come on now, you know the shoes complete the outfit," said Tyrone.

"Yeah you're right" said Jackson, "But please be careful"

"Don't walk like you normally walk, try and hi step so you don't scuff my shoes."

Jackson walked toward the closet, "How do you want to accent the suit? "

"Do you want blue and black, or blue and white or blue on blue?"

"I have three different pairs of shoes to match that suit," said Jackson.

"Can I try on all three combinations to see which one looks the best?" Tyrone asked.

"After you wash your ass you can the towels are in the linen closet," said Jackson.

"One more thing, "Tyrone paused, "I need some clean underclothes".

"Man have you lost your rabbit ass mind?"

"Aint nobody wearing my draws," said Jackson.

"I know you don't want me to put the same old dirty ones I have on again, and then put on your nice new suit, do you" asked Tyrone.

"Tyrone, man you sure are asking a lot," said Jackson.

"Come on now, you don't expect me to put on this fly ass suit with some dirty draws do you," asked Tyrone? Pointing to the tall dresser next to the bed Jackson said, "There should be a few pair of brand new T-shirts and boxers in the top left drawer."

"I'm going in the other bedroom to finish getting dressed call me when you're ready".

Heading into the other bedroom Jackson stopped and turned to say with a smile.

"You, Trouble, and Bullethead have been bugging me all night to get ready,"

"And you end up being the last one to get dressed, imagine that".

As Tyrone jumped in the shower his mind began to picture the response Jackson always got when he entered the club. He tried to imagine how it felt to be so popular with the ladies. After tonight he promised himself he would get it together. He wanted a new wardrobe, to help improve his player statues.

Tyrone was also anticipating the evening with Tamika. He knew that the outfit Jackson loaned him would do the trick. Tyrone after showering dried his body and began to get dressed.

"Jackson, can you come here for a minute," yelled Tyrone?

"Yeah man" Jackson said, as he strolled around the corner.

"I need one more thing," said Tyrone. Starting to get irritated Jackson said, "What now Tyrone?"

"I need some smell good to complete the total package."

"But I want to spray it on my body instead of on the suit, so I don't stain the silk."

"Smart thinking Tyrone you know you might have some potential after all," said Jackson.

"Jackson I'm going to be so smooth, I'll dazzle all the honnies tonight," said Tyrone.

"Tyrone just be yourself." "People like when a person doesn't change."

"Just do and say what you normally would," "You'll get a better response trust me."

"Tyrone you already have a nice, smooth, mellow groove about yourself."

"So relax and just be yourself, you feel me," said Jackson?

"Yeah I feel you Jackson." "I guess I'm nervous about meeting Tamika."

"I just want to make a good impression on her."

"From your description of her she sounds cold blooded."

"I don't have the same success with the ladies the way you do."

"Don't get me wrong I get my share,"

"But the caliber of women you meet far exceeds almost everybody else we know."

"I don't mean to be on your dick, but the truth is the truth."

"I give props where props are due," if I didn't give props where props are due."

"Then that would make me a hater,"

"I will never hate on a person I consider a friend," "You feel me Jackson?"

"Tyrone thanks for the compliment, but right now it's time to do the dam thing."

"Finished getting dressed so we can have a drink together"

"I want to toast to our friendship." "Cool that sounds good to me Jackson," said Tyrone.

"But remember I told you the henny was almost gone," said Tyrone.

"No problem," said Jackson. "I always keep a little something for entertaining the honnies."

"When you finished getting dressed come down stairs."

While Jackson headed into the other bedroom to finished getting dressed the phone began to ring,   "Hey Tyrone can you please get the phone."

"Sure," said Tyrone. Grabbing the phone he said "Hello." On the other end the sexiest voice he had ever heard came back to him.

"Hey baby," "I just called to let you know I was on my way." "Excuse me," said Tyrone?

"This is Tamika whom am I speaking to?"

"I'm sorry baby you must have thought I was Jackson."

"He's still getting dressed." "Can I take a message for him?"

"Yes," "Can you tell him Tamika is on the way over there?"

"Sure, do you mind if I make a comment," asked Tyrone?

"No," said Tamika. "Tamika you have the sexiest voice I've ever heard in my life."

"Thank you," said Tamika, "What is your name?"

"I'm sorry," "I was being rude my name is Tyrone."

"I'm one of Jackson's friends."

"Tamika if you look anything like you sound,"

"Then baby you must be a dime piece," said Tyrone.

"A what piece," asked Tamika?

"Excuse me for being ghetto but a dime piece to the fellows in the hood is an attractive woman."

"A perfect ten," explained Tyrone.

Tamika stated, "I've never heard a compliment like that before."

"But thank you."

"You're welcome," said Tyrone; "I'll give Jackson the message, bye Tamika."

Hanging up the phone Tyrone yelled; "Hey Jackson that was Tamika on the phone."

"She said she was on her way over here."

Jackson yelled back "Cool, now it's on and popping baby." As Jackson finished getting dressed he began to wonder if Tamika and Tyrone would really hit it off.

He began to compare in his mind their interest, and their personalities. Then a smile formed on his lips, "Yep it's a perfect match."

"There is no way I can be wrong on this one baby," He said to himself.

Jackson yelled to Tyrone, "Let me have a look at you for a final inspection."

Chapter Eight

Tyrone came strolling around the corner and asked Jackson, "What do you think?"

Jackson was caught off guard for a moment. After regaining his composure he stated,

"Dam baby, you sure look good."

"If I didn't know you, I would swear up and down you were a player."

"Tyrone you are cleaner than skeeters peter."

"There is no way a woman would say no to you tonight for anything", "You feel me?"

Tyrone smiled from ear to ear dam near showing every tooth in his mouth. As the thought of meeting Tamika crossed Tyrone's mind.

The smile slowly turned to a real concern.

"Jackson do you really think Tamika will be interested in me?"

"From what I see standing before me, there's no way you can lose."

"I'm not just saying that to make you feel good either."

"Come on now baby pull it together."

"This doesn`t sound like the Tyrone I know."

"Man just be yourself and you`ll be fine."

"If I didn't think you had some game about yourself."

"Then I would not have wasted my time fixing you up, you feel me?"

"Don't start simping, when you should be pimping," said Jackson.

"Tyrone let`s go have that drink so you can relax a little."

"You are all uptight for nothing."

"Don't start that gay shit on me tonight."

Jackson began to laugh so Tyrone could relax. He knew by picking with him. It would bring out his game to counter act what he was saying to him.

Whistling as they headed down stairs Jackson began to think how he would leave Tyrone and Tamika alone to get to know one another. He knew he had a minute to get his plan together because Tamika lived an hour away.

Heading into the kitchen Jackson went to his secret stash to retrieve another bottle of henny.

"Here you go player, get busy, getting busy," said Jackson.

"Man you know I need some ice."

"I don't mess around with this shit straight."

"Because I know what henny can do to a person,"

"When I took that shower it took away my buzz."

"But I know soon as I start back drinking."

"My buzz will come right back," said Tyrone.

"Well I need a good drink."

"So make my first two a shot straight out the neck," said Jackson,

"Since you have a head start," "I'm trying to catch up." Pouring their drinks, Tyrone put his glass to Jackson`s and began to toast.

"Chedonnie." "What did you just toast to Tyrone," asked Jackson? Tyrone began to explain, that it meant one hundred years of success in Italian.

"That sounds good to me."

"But let me add my own little toast to that."

"Keep pimping, never simping, peace and love, forever to my niggas, you feel me?"

"I feel you baby," said Tyrone.

Turning up the glass to drain all of its contents, Jackson swallowed it all in one gulp.

"That's what I'm talking about baby."

"Take that shit right to the head, like a soldier."

"Pour me another shot," "Then I can start sipping on some ice."

Tyrone poured Jackson a second shot.

Downing the shot, Jackson said, "Tyrone change that cd."

"I want to hear some party music."

"What cd do you want me to put in the disc player," asked Tyrone? Pointing to the cd rack, Jackson said, "There should be a mixed cd on the very top."

"Play that one because it's bumping."

The two shots of henny Jackson had drank were starting to take effect on him. Now Jackson was now in the party mood.

Jackson thought to himself "I got my homeboy looking good and smelling good."

"I'm looking good and smelling good."

"We are drinking right, and we have a beautiful honnie on the way, tonight just might turn out alright."

As Jackson was sitting there plotting his getaway. He remembered he and Tyrone were going to ride to the club with Trouble and Bullethead.

But since they bailed out on them he was trying to figure out how he would get to the club without having to drive himself that would have to be the very last resort.

Then he remembered, he did invite Tamika to go have a drink with him, and some friends. So Jackson figured, why not let her and Tyrone take him to the club, and leave him there.

At the club he knew he could always get a ride home.

Jackson started to picture the attention he would receive as he would enter the club, and it brought a smile to his face.

He thought in his mind about all the different outfits he had already worn, "They`ve already seen me in the pretty in pink," "The money green, the beautiful blue, and the gorgeous grey".

"Now I'm going to kill them with this canary yellow."

Jackson stood up to walk to the full length mirror to check himself to make sure every detail was complete.

First he examined his hair slowly sliding his eyes over every inch of hair making sure not a one was out of place.

He said to himself "Check that definitely is official."

Allowing his eyes to slowly examine his facial hair, Jackson began to turn his head from side to side matching every point, making sure everything was even Steven.

He reached down on to the table grabbing a small comb to check the thickness of his beard, and mustache. You never want them to thick just in case you have to kiss a honnie.

A woman doesn't like a brillo pad rubbing up against her skin. They want something soft like a fury little stuffed animal to tickle their face and other areas. So checking the thickness and softness makes a difference.

Jackson thought to himself if a player doesn't have pride in his appearance, then he ain`t a player. He began to examine the brightness of his white shirt in the light.

He took his eyes over every inch of the collar making sure the shirt had that brand new right out of the package cleanliness. Next he examined his Armani silk tie. He checked to make sure the tie didn't have those already tied tie lines in it.

Jackson's philosophy was if you're going to look the part, look the part all the way, you shouldn't half step. Jackson thought in his mind it doesn't take but a minute to run a warm iron over your tie while you're ironing your shirt, because to him the smallest detail mattered.

He had seen cats who in their own minds thought they were shit sharp.

But they didn't do the final examination and was always short somewhere.

They would approach a woman thinking they would get their Mack on and the woman would be doing the final inspection for him, to see how tight his game really was.

See what most dudes don't realize is this that first slick line that a man spits at a woman only gets her attention. From there on she's not listening to you until she inspects you from head to toe.

So if your game is not all the way tight, any woman who has some game about herself will expose any flaws or weakness in your game.

To a real woman part of a man's game is his appearance, so if your flawed stepping to a woman, she'll peep it out.

Now if she will pull your coat to the fact or not is something different, that's why if a man gets a woman to chill with him ten out of ten times in his mind, he thought he macked her.

But the truth be told either she felt sorry for him, and gave him some holler. Or she was lonely and didn't want to go home from the club alone.

As she might have done a hundred times prior to meeting him, or the broad just might be horny. I mean they have needs too and she might just want her needs fulfilled that night.

Because a lot a dudes don't really have game their whole game consists of eating pussy.

They will eat some pussy in order to get some pussy. Now tell me where is the game in that you feel me?

That's not representing been a player, that's simping not pimping. Jackson began to smile thinking of all the guys he watched strike out talking to different women in the club.

He would sit at the bar, sipping on some henny just observing his surroundings.

He watched all the fake players or want to B's step up to the plate and strike out. It wasn't their dress, no let me take that back part of it was the way they dressed.

Jackson thought to himself, it was a lack of confidence.

If a man can't look a woman in her eyes, and tell her what's on his mind.

Then that man has absolutely no confidence whatsoever. And a woman can spot a guy with no confidence a mile away.

Also most guys try and be what they think that woman wants them to be instead of being themselves. Jackson thought in his mind that is a lame with a capitol L.

Then he would watch all the so called big spenders.

Now if that same dude came into the bar, and didn`t buy everybody drinks. Would he still get that same attention?

Would those same old broke chicks sit around and listen to his lame ass stories, and lies. The big spenders buy attention because they have a lack of confidence. If you don't believe me, sit and watch any guy who buys drinks all night.

After he's spent all his money see how all the attention leaves from around him.

If a person has charisma and a charming disposition then the money in its self would not be the main factor commanding the attention.

His sheer presence would be enough.

But in a lot of cases the money hides another case of being a lame; it's just a lame with money.

Jackson thought about himself he thought let me analyze myself for a minute.

Do I buy people drinks just to get attention?

He thought now why do I buy people drinks, he questioned himself? I buy friends drinks that would do the same for me.

He thought about the lean times when he would look good, but was flat broke.

Those same men and women would do the same for him. So in his mind he knew he wasn't trying to buy attention.

Then Jackson thought about his confidence level.

In his mind he thought that's not an option, it was part of his personality. It just was second nature to stand up and be a man with confidence.

He loved looking in to a woman's eyes, and saying something smooth to her to see if he could make her smile. He was taught at an early age to always look a person in their eyes when speaking to them.

Jackson thought to himself how some guys fear talking to a woman.

How can a person fear something they desire? That's almost like dying of starvation and being afraid to eat.

In Jackson's mind he thought how blessed he was to have a strong mind.

Still gazing into the mirror Jackson continued his inspection of himself. Jackson turned to one side, looking at how his Jacket fit his body.

Jackson began to check how the lines of the suit flowed, flowing smoothly over every contour of his body. Next he examined the seams and creases of his slacks.

Jackson growing up was told make your creases sharp enough to cut your finger on them.

He thought in his mind that's where the saying man you sure are sharp might have originated.

It just seemed like it made sense, most ghetto cliché's had some truth to them.

Jackson allowed his eyes to follow the sharp creases down to what he thought was the clincher to the package his hi steppers, the now a later gators. In the final inspection the shoes are what make you or break you.

Have you ever seen a person wearing a bomb ass outfit, and you start to admire them for looking good. You just casually admire their hair.

In your mind you say that they look good they got it together. Then your eyes slide down to the rest of the body.

You allow your eyes to see how their outfit fits them, there is nothing worse than to see a person with an, I can't breathe outfit on.

An outfit so tight you wonder how they got into it. It's seems like the person is just too cheap to go shopping.

Most people blow up when they grow up so get in where you fit in, and stop trying to look young. That's a ghetto expression for stop wearing tight clothes.

Now if the outfit is flowing on their body correctly. Then the clincher is at hand what kind of shoes they picked out to complete their outfit. This will either elevate them over the top, or send them crashing to the dirt.

There is nothing worse than to see a person with some crazy ass shoes that have nothing to do with what their wearing.

Picture a man with a nice conservative dark blue suit. It's a traditional classic that anybody can wear. And look good with either brown shoes, black shoes, or blue shoes. Now to save my life why would a person put on some red shoes?

It could not be because they thought they were styling and profiling.

Jackson thought that's just the lameness coming out in a person. They tried to be cool and took it as far as they could.

Before they reverted back to the original, which is being a lame.

Jackson's confidence level began to shoot up through the roof as he completed his examination of himself.

In a vain, cocky smirk he whispered "Dam you look good."

With the knowledge of being complete, he strolled back into the sitting room with Tyrone.

Tyrone asked, "Jackson how are you feeling?" Because he wanted to judge how he thought the night would go from Jackson's response.

Jackson responded, "I'm cooler than a fan baby; you dig."

"Tyrone it won't ever get much better than this."

"I got my best friend chillin with me."

"We're dressed to impress, and a pocket full of money, what else could you ask for."

"By the way Jackson"

Tyrone interrupted, "I might need to borrow a few green backs."

Jackson responded, "Tyrone don't worry about it I got you, tonight is on me."

"But remember don't make a habit of this, you feel me?"

"I feel you," said Tyrone.

Jackson looking at his watch, said "Pass me the henny."

Tyrone leaned over stretching out his arm extending the bottle over to Jackson asked, "What time is it anyway?"

"It's time for you to meet the finest woman you ever will meet." A huge smile formed on Jackson's face as he made the statement to Tyrone.

Chapter Nine

Pouring himself a stiff drink Jackson waited for Tyrone's response, glancing out of the corner of his eye while turning up his glass.

Jackson paused at the look that was on Tyrone's face. It was a look he had seen a thousand times before it was the look of fear. He would watch the other guys try and spit game at women, and he would notice fear on their faces.

Jackson thought how funny it was to see guys trying to spit game and be petrified at the same time. But he had never noticed that look on Tyrone's face before.

Jackson thought he was imagining it for a second.

He put down his glass, and began to joke with Tyrone. "I know you aint scared," asked Jackson?

"Naw man, me scared, scared of what a honnie;"

"You should know me better than that."

The cold feeling of fear engulfed Tyrone's whole body, he couldn't hide it anymore. Jackson began to feel a real concern for his friend.

So he decided to try and boost his confidence.

"Come on player pull it together."

"Tyrone go look in the mirror and tell me what you see."

Slowly rising to his feet Tyrone casually strolled to the hallway mirror.

Jackson asked, "Now what do you see?"

Tyrone glanced at himself from head to toe and said, "I see what I always see,"

"A decent looking young black man trying to get in where I fit in."

"But tonight is different Jackson."

"I see me wearing your suit, trying to be you."

"The only difference is, I'm not you."

"I'm not weak or anything."

"But I don't have the same success with the ladies the way you do."

"And to meet one of your ex`s on a blind date is a little scary."

"Even though I'm dressed like you, I'm not you."

"She might like the way I look tonight, but what about tomorrow?"

"When I put on my own clothes and just be me, then what?"

"Will this woman still like the regular old Tyrone?"

"I don't have a big nice house, or a fancy car, or the sharp ass clothes."

"Will she still like me when I'm not trying to be you?"

"I just think she might be expecting a guy similar to you."

"You feel me Jackson?"

"Tyrone this woman is not like that."

"She is looking for someone to settle down with."

"If I thought she wouldn't have any holler for you."

"Then I never would have called her, you feel me?"

"Yeah I feel you Jackson, but I'm still nervous."

"I just think Tamika might be expecting a guy like you," "Because most people associate with people that are similar to themselves."

"People hang together who have the same amount of money."

"Rich people hang out with rich people,"

"And likewise for people that are socially accepted they run in the same circles with people that are socially acceptable,"

"Last but not least people who have the same believes associate with one another."

"Whether financial, social or spiritual, birds of a feather flock together,"

"Since most women know you're a player."

"They might expect all of the people you associate with, to be players too."

"Tyrone calm down and try to relax."

"You're getting all nervous for nothing."

"Tamika is just a woman she's just like every other woman you've ever met in your life."

"Tyrone I'm going to tell you a secret," "The secret why I have so much success with women."

"I learned a long time ago from watching the OG`s, and listening to them that every woman is the same."

"People will argue with you about that every time a person says it, but it's true."

"If you don't believe me check this out."

"What is the main thing every woman desires from a man?"

Tyrone looking at Jackson began to shrug his shoulders, and said," I don't know." Jackson moved to the very edge of the couch and looked intently at Tyrone and began to say.

"Every woman first and foremost wants a man to be able to communicate with."

"Women feel the need to express themselves through their conversation."

"So if a woman feels she can talk to you,"

"Then she feels she can express her deepest feelings to you,"

"By expressing their deepest feelings to you," "She feels she can open up her heart to you, you feel me?"

"If a woman has opened her heart to you this to them is more meaningful than sex."

"So for her to give her body to a man it's just a natural extension of her feelings."

"That's why sex to a woman is not just a physical act it's an extension of her mind,"

"And a piece of her heart," "That's why woman don't say come sleep with me, or fuck me, they say come and make love to me."

"A woman that has decided to give her body to a man has decided that man has the criteria to fulfill her heart."

Tyrone stared at Jackson in amazement. All the years he had known Jackson he had never heard him speak like this before.

Tyrone asked Jackson, "So what about the women who want money?"

Jackson began to answer the question but paused for a second; because he didn't want to give Tyrone mixed signals.

Because the women Jackson was speaking about were the women who hold the title of being women, What Tyrone didn't understand was not all females are women.

Jackson decided to make it plain as he could, so there wouldn't be any misunderstandings. "Every creatures main issue is survival, meaning you use all of your abilities to try and preserve your existence."

"Case in point, if a person namely a female is lacking in some area to preserve her survival."

"They will compensate, by using some other area they feel adequate, to equal out their short coming."

"By using what they think is a commodity to achieve their survival."

"What did you just say asked Tyrone?"

"In short they will use anything they think a man wants to receive money"

"Which is what they think will continue their survival."

"Because they're not able to do it themselves either from a lack of education, a lack skill or just plain lazy."

"Some women are weak when it comes to them maintaining themselves with just every day basic living."

"So if they see potential in a man that they feel is strong, and confident."

"They will latch on to him to try and have that man care for them."

"In any way they feel is necessary." "And in turn they are willing to supply him with the cooking of his meals, cleaning, and sex."

"They are willing to do whatever they feel is adequate compensation for his financial support." "A lot of that stems from a poor upbringing."

"Their parents never instilled the proper tools for them to be able to survive."

"A lot of parents feel like if they had to endure certain hardships to learn survival."

"Then they don't want to make it easier for their kids," "Which to me is bullshit, but to each his own."

"Because when they get old the same child they neglected." "Will be the same child they will be looking to for support."

"That's why you see so many old people in nursing homes dying of loneliness."

"On the other hand you have people who had it rough growing up that over compensate," "And never give the child room to grow," "By trying to shelter them from life."

"Which in most cases makes them dependent people" "That will latch on to anything, and everything to try and maintain their survival."

"But enough about that, I want you to calm down, and enjoy whatever happens, you feel me?"

"I feel you; but dam I never knew you were so deep."

"Why haven't we had a conversation like that before?" Tyrone was so taken back by Jackson's words that he completely forgot the fear he was feeling earlier.

Chapter Ten

As Tyrone strolled back from the hallway to the sitting room his confidence began to rise, and all the anxiety he was feeling quickly dissipated. Tyrone looking over at Jackson began to smile, and said, "Pass me the bottle." "Now I'm ready to kick it."

Tyrone poured two drinks, and passed one to Jackson. He began to toast to Jackson. While lifting his glass high in the air Tyrone said, "Thank you for being a real friend, may god bless you in all aspects of your life."

Finishing his toast Jackson drank his drink and sat down to ponder what was just said.

"Tyrone did you really mean what you just said?"

Tyrone staring Jackson in his eyes said "Yes." "I'm not on no gay shit."

"But if I feel you're really my friend." "Then why wouldn't I want God to fulfill your hearts desires?"

"What person doesn't want the very best for their friends?"

"But I think with us it goes beyond friendship."

"I consider you to be just like the brother I never had."

"Just like tonight most so called friends would of never went out of their way to fix me up with one of their ex women."

"Most guys feel like if they slept with that woman."

"Then they don't want anyone they know to holler at that woman."

"But you had my best interest at heart" "Which is the same thing I toasted too for you."

"And you went a step farther." "You just didn't say hey this is Tamika and this is Tyrone and walk away."

"You let me borrow this bad ass suit," "These sharp ass shoes," "Not to mention the draws and t-shirt". "Not too many people would have gone that extra mile for a friend, you feel me?"

"Now do you understand the toast?"

"But it just didn't start tonight you have always looked out for me, even when we were little."

"You never asked if I was wrong or right you were there to have my back every time I needed you."

"Tonight I just want to say thank you."

"You're welcome," said Jackson.

"Ok enough of that mushy stuff; Tamika should be pulling up at any minute."

"So what club were you planning on going to tonight," asked Tyrone?

Jackson said," I was thinking about the warehouse." "I haven't been there in a few months."

"I was thinking we should go there because they have three different floors of music." "They have jazz on the first floor, R&B on the second floor and old school hip hop on the top floor."

"So whatever mood you're in you can still kick it there, you feel me?"

Tyrone looked at Jackson and said, "A nice little quiet table in the corner on the jazz floor sounds good to me."

"Then I can still talk to Tamika," "I won't have to holler for her to hear me"

"We can order some wine to sip on, and discuss our interest, you feel me?"

Tyrone extended his fist to give Jackson a fist, to fist pound with a kool aid smile back on his face.

In a slow drawn out fashion, Tyrone said, "I'm back."

"Jackson man I don't know why I was tripping earlier."

"But now, I'm back on the attack, giving my Mack without any slack, you feel me, baby boy."

Jackson could just laugh. "Now that's the Tyrone I know right there."

Jackson stood up to give Tyrone five, as they were laughing and joking the doorbell rang. The surprise of the doorbell startled Tyrone.

Tyrone looked at Jackson with a surprised look on his face. Smiling back at Tyrone Jackson said,

"Now I wonder who that could be."

Jackson's comment made Tyrone want to get his composure together. Tyrone looked at Jackson and said, "Let me get the door."

Rising to his feet, Tyrone strolled to the hallway stopping in front of the full length mirror. Just to do one last inspection to boost his confidence.

While staring in the mirror he slowing rubbed his hand over his mustache down to his beard. Tyrone said to himself "Be on the attack, giving your Mack, without any slack."

With his inspection complete he moved with confidence toward the front door. Slowly he opened the door to greet who he assumed was Tamika on the other side.

As the door slowly opened revealing Tamika's full appearance. Tyrone's eyes instantly locked with Tamika's. For what seemed like a full minute. Tamika quickly dropped her eyes to pretend like she was being shy.

But in reality she was inspecting Tyrone. She slowly inspected the style of shoes he was wearing. She wanted to see if he was broke and wearing cheap shoes. Tamika smiled to herself seeing the gators he wore were in perfect condition.

She also noticed Tyrone was wearing a size thirteen. She slowly followed the creases of his slacks toward his crotch.

Trying to see a bulge or an outline imprint of the size of his dick, or his bank roll to her either one would satisfy her. If his dick was small and he had money she would work with him. Tamika slowly followed the lines of Tyrone's suit jacket up to his broad shoulders, pausing inspecting his chest.

With a smile of approval she lifted her eyes to once again to meet his.

Tyrone being naive asked, "I know you're not shy are you?"

Tamika while smiling from ear to ear played along and said, "A little bit"

Tyrone extended his hand and trying to muster up all the bass he could in his voice said,

"Hi I`m Tyrone."

"I'm that guy you spoke to earlier on the telephone."

"It's nice to meet you Tyrone; by the way my name is Tamika."

"Do you still think I'm a dime piece," asked Tamika?

Tyrone still taken aback by her beauty could only smile and couldn't really answer the question.

Sliding to the side, and extending his hand, while bowing his head as to greet royalty.

Tyrone said, "Excuse for being rude please come in."

Tamika gracefully slid pass Tyrone, the perfume she was wearing engulfed Tyrone's senses, hypnotizing his mind into submission.

Closing the door, Tyrone followed close behind Tamika into the sitting room like a dog being lead on a leash.

As Tamika came around the corner Jackson stood up to greet her with a Hugh bear hug.

"Hey baby it's good to see you," said Jackson.

"It's been a while," said Tamika.

Holding Tamika's hand, Jackson slowly began to turn Tamika admiring her beauty from head to toe.

"Baby I don't know why I waited so long to see you."

"By the way this is a very, good friend of mine, his name is Tyrone"

Tyrone stood and watched Jackson hug Tamika. A sense of jealousy came over him. But then he remembered Jackson had called Tamika for him, and not to holler at her.

Regaining his composure, Tyrone said, "Hi again, and told Jackson he had already introduced himself at the door."

Tyrone asked Tamika, "Would you like a drink?"

"What do you have," she asked?

"We have Hennessey or wine."

"I'll take a glass of wine."

Tyrone motioned to Jackson to come into the kitchen with him. Once in the kitchen, Tyrone threw his arm over Jackson's shoulder and said, "Man you weren't lying when you said she was beautiful."

"Let me tell you a secret when I saw you hug Tamika a feeling of jealousy came over me."

With his arm still around Jackson's shoulders .Tyrone took his other hand and playfully punched Jackson in the stomach.

Starting to laugh at Tyrone's comment. Jackson said, "I told you she was straight, didn't I"?

Sliding his arm from around Jackson's neck, and shoulders. Tyrone walked over to the cabinet to get the wine and looked for some wine glasses for Tamika to drink out of.

While opening the bottle of wine, Tyrone said, "I had to check myself real quick"

"We just had a conversation saying how we had each other's back,"

"Then instantly I felt that feeling hit me."

"But I shook it off, I told myself check yourself, before you wreck yourself," "You feel me?"

"I feel you," said Jackson, "But think about this for a minute."

"If I was going to holler at Tamika again,"

"How would it benefit me, by adding someone else into the mix, you feel me?"

Tyrone asked Jackson, "Do you have any wine glasses?"

Pointing to the middle cabinet Jackson said, "Yes their in there."

Tyrone opened the cabinet and grabbed three glasses.

While looking at Jackson, Tyrone said, "Let's have another toast." Grabbing the bottle of wine Tyrone followed Jackson back into the sitting room.

Tyrone poured everyone a drink and said, "I would like to toast to having good friends and enjoying tonight to the fullest."

"Preach brother preach" Jackson added to the toast.

Then in a sexy smirk Tamika said, "Yes indeed," and they touched glasses and drained the contents.

"Woo wee that wine always goes right to my head," said Tamika, as she sat her glass down to catch her breath.

"Tyrone can you pour me another drink?"

Tyrone grabbed the bottle and said, "Are you sure you want another drink?"

"You just said that it went right to your head."

"I don't want you to think I'm trying to get you drunk to take advantage of you."

Smiling, Tamika said, "Don't worry about me I'm a big girl."

"I can handle whatever you got baby boy."

Tyrone grabbed the glass and only poured a small amount for Tamika to sip on. Extending the glass back to Tamika Tyrone said, "Here baby, how's that?"

Grabbing the glass Tamika drank the wine in one gulp. She said, "I already know you're a nice guy,"

"Because if you weren't you wouldn't be here."

"So treat me like I'm a big girl and stop trying to baby me."

"I want to kick it the same as you do, and as Jackson would say, you feel me?" They all laughed and got down to the business of kicking it.

After a couple more bottles of wine. Jackson said, "Let's call a cab so we can go out for a while."

Tyrone said, "That sounds good to me."

"Because I want to get this sexy thing on the dance floor,"

"To see if she can work, you feel me homeboy?"

Giving Jackson a fist to fist pound Tyrone stood up to go to the restroom and said,

"Please excuse me" "I'll be right back."

After Tyrone left the room Tamika looked at Jackson and said, "You didn't say anything about my outfit."

"Do you like it?"

Tamika stood up to show Jackson the dress she was wearing. She slowly turned in a small circle showing every inch of her body.

"So what do you think?"

Jackson began to look at Tamika the way he did when he first met her.

"Baby you know I always was attracted to you."

"Come to think about it. That's the same dress you wore on our first date."

Jackson got a hard on remembering how good her pussy was.

"Baby I called you tonight to meet Tyrone"

"But my dick is getting hard for you baby."

Tamika smiled and said, "Is it baby?"

"Show it to me so I can taste you."

"As a matter of fact my pussy is soaking wet for you."

"I've been wet ever since you called me."

"I was thinking you just wanted to share me with you friend."

"Because no other females were here,"

"I thought about it, and I decided I'll do anything you ask me to do tonight"

Tamika sat on the edge of the couch, and pulled her dress up to her stomach and said,

"Give me your hand I want you to feel how hot, and wet I am."

Opening her long muscular legs she exposed a shaved pussy with a throbbing, hard clitoris.

Jackson could see the insides of her thighs were soaking wet.

He slowly slid over to her and began to caress her pussy, sliding his fingers deep inside of her.

Tamika began to moan and nibble on his ears every word she moaned she blew her hot breath on Jackson's neck making him want her even more.

Tamika kept repeating the same thing over and over.

"I want you to fuck my mouth, then my pussy, and then my ass."

"Come on and give it to me baby."

Suddenly Jackson stopped he had gone too far. Pulling his fingers from inside of her Jackson realized Tamika had an orgasm while he was forcing his fingers deep inside of her.

Pulling away from her Jackson said, "That was not my intention baby; I didn't call you over for that."

"I want you to get to know Tyrone."

"He really is a nice guy."

"He's someone that will love you the way you always talked about."

"I think if you make an effort both of you can be very happy together."

Looking into Jackson's eyes Tamika asked, "What's wrong, why you don't like me anymore?"

"Baby it's not like that at all."

"I just want you to have the whole package."

"I mean not just for a little while"

"Not until you get tired of me, or I get tired of you."

"But the kind of love where you don't have to wonder about that person when they're not with you."

"When you see them you smile, because you're happy to see them."

"Someone that compliments you as a person, a person to give you security"

"Somebody you can spiritually connect with, and grow old together, you feel me?"

"I'm talking about finally finding real love."

"The kind of love only god can bless you with."

"So go wash up in the bathroom in my bedroom."

"There are washcloths and towels in the linen closet."

Jackson kissed her on cheek and sent her to freshen up.

Chapter Eleven

As Jackson was thinking about what just happened. Tyrone came around the corner, and asked, "Where's Tamika did she leave?"

"No you were taking too long in the bathroom, so she went upstairs to use it."

While Jackson was speaking to Tyrone he slowly eased into the restroom to wash his hands. Tyrone followed Jackson into the restroom and said. "I don't know why but, I have a feeling something just happened."

"I don't know what but I have this feeling in my gut."

"Would you like to tell me or do you want me to guess?"

"Nothing happened the way you might be thinking."

"We just had a talk, and I told her to put a little effort into getting to know you."

Washing away the evidence Jackson thought it best not to tell Tyrone everything because he wanted him to feel confident about his chances with Tamika. While drying his hands, Jackson asked Tyrone if he was ready to go out.

Walking around the corner they merged back into the sitting room with Tamika. She said, "I think I'd better go I don't feel like going out now."

"I think I drank too much wine."

Tyrone gave Jackson an angry look. Jackson just shrugged his shoulders as to say, "I don't know what's going on." Tyrone began to ask Tamika, what he could do to change her mind, and what he could do to comfort her. Tamika looking past Tyrone began to read Jackson's lips.

Jackson silently formed the words saying, "Please just try, if you don't like him."

"I'll make it up to you I promise."

With the offer Jackson just presented to Tamika. She was happy all over again. Tyrone with his back toward Jackson couldn't see the offer Jackson had made to Tamika.

Tyrone thought in his mind I'll do whatever it takes to try and build a friendship with Tamika. Tyrone and Jackson had been friends ever since grade school and always looked out for one another. But now that Tyrone felt this desire for Tamika the years of friendship seemed trivial.

Tamika looked at Tyrone and gave him a friendly smile, and asked, "Are you ready to go to the club?" "I'm feeling better now so we don't need to call a cab."

"I can drive us there," said Tamika.

Feeling a since of relieve Tyrone smiled and said, "Yes I would love to go with you anywhere you would like to go."

Tyrone extended his elbow to Tamika so he could walk her to the car. Tyrone thought about the things that Jackson told him about Tamika and what she had been through in her past relationships and he decided to be a perfect gentleman.

Tyrone was careful with every gesture and every response, as they got into the car to leave.

Jackson walked around to the passenger side back seat, to give Tyrone, and Tamika a chance to talk as they rode to the club. Slowly In a friendly type way, Tamika began to warm up to Tyrone.

She thought in her mind there was nothing wrong with being his friend; after all he was being the perfect gentleman.

As Tamika turned the key to start the car, Jackson said, "Let me go and make sure I locked the door."

Easing out the car, Jackson caught Tyrone's eye in the mirror and gave him the wink, meaning I told you it was on.

As the powerful motor turned over in the caddy the smooth sounds of an old favorite came drifting in.

The words of the song said, Hi my name is Larry and I like a woman who loves everything and everybody, and if you feel that this is you, then this is what I want you to do.

Tyrone mimicking the words to the song extended his hand repeating the words that played on the radio.

The song said; take my hand come with me baby, to love land. Let me show you how sweet it could be, sharing your love with Larry Listen, float, float on.

Tyrone while grabbing Tamika's hand begun singing the words of the song adding all the feeling he could muster.

Tyrone was trying to show how much he truly meant what he was repeating from the words of the song. Tyrone thought by replacing the name Larry, with his name, that Tamika might get the message that he was trying to convey to her through the words of the song that was being sung.

Tyrone thought the gestures he was making were very smooth and subtle.

But Tamika could tell when she had caught a big fish. Ever since she was very young, men would try and give hints and suggestions instead of just saying what was really on their minds.

Over the years she had learned to play along she thought it was amusing to make a game out of their fear.

They were afraid to say what they really wanted so she would act dumb and play her game.

But she knew what they really wanted she would try her best to get the men to express what was on their minds.

She would say things like if you tell me what's on your mind I'll tell you what's on my mind in a very seductive way.

She would insinuate she was interested just to get them to confess their deepest desires. She had gotten so good at it she was better than a lot of higher priced attorneys.

Once the confession was made, the game was over. She would say things like "If you told me your intentions up front then it would have been fine." "But since I had to pry it out of you, then I don't think it will work."

"I need a man that can express whatever is on his mind, and not be afraid."

"How would it benefit me to be with a man that is afraid of me?"

"I need a man to be a man."

As Tamika watched Tyrone singing she decided not to hurt him just yet, because she was trying to show Jackson she was giving Tyrone a chance. Tamika reached, and turned the radio down to a whisper, and she asked Tyrone what were his intentions for her.

Once the words had come out of her mouth she tried in her mind to retrieve them, but it was too late she had put the game into play.

Tyrone looked at Tamika for a few seconds and, staring into her eyes he asked, "Do you want the truth?"

Tamika with a look of intrigue said "Yes, the truth would be nice."

Tyrone turned his head toward the window as if he was pleading his case to an unseen person, slowly he began to speak.

Almost as to show he was ashamed of what he was about to say.

Tyrone began saying, "Earlier today I hooked up with Jackson."

"We decided that we were on a pussy hunt for this evening"

"We were supposed to ride to the club with some other cats."

" But that fell through," "So I assumed the night was over."

"So my main man Jackson suggested that I meet you."

"At first he was telling me I got the perfect woman for you type shit."

"In my mind, I was saying yeah right."

"So He called you and hooked it up."

"So I was like, I'll ride just to see where this might go, just for the hell of it, you feel me?"

"When I spoke to you on the phone, you sparked my interest a little more"

"Your voice had beauty in it."

"I know it sounds crazy to say that."

"But I could hear beauty in your voice."

"So at that point I decided to investigate a little deeper."

"I inquired a few things about you from Jackson."

"I still didn't have enough information to go on."

"So I decided that since my interest was sparked," "I would put my best foot forward and just see where it might go, you feel me?"

"When I answered the door and seen you face to face."

"Your beauty over whelmed me."

"From the moment our eyes met I decided I would not play any games."

"I would be myself come hell or high water."

"I also wanted to see you twirk that fat ass." Tyrone said, with a smile to lighten things up. Tamika was so impressed that Tyrone told her the truth without having to twist his arm.

She decided she would open up and give Tyrone more than just an average chance.

Tyrone spoke up breaking the silence that crept into the car after his confession.

"What do you think happened to Jackson?"

"He's been gone for a while I think I'd better go check on him to see if he's ok."

Opening the car door, Tyrone began to ponder whether or not he should have confessed. Then he thought about the words Jackson kept saying to him earlier. Just be yourself, and people will love you, you feel me?

Tyrone full of confidence now was truly at the top of his game. Which when you look at it is cool, because Tyrone's game consisted of him just being who he is a cool down to earth brother.

As Tyrone approached the front door, he could see Jackson on the phone with his back to the door struck in a pose of deep conversation.

Tyrone slid through the cracked door and walked over to Jackson, tapping him on the shoulder.

"Is everything alright?"

"We were getting worried about you, because you were taking so long."

Turning with a surprised look, Jackson smiled, seeing it was Tyrone, and not Tamika that was tapping him on the shoulder.

He was so engulfed in the conversation didn't hear Tyrone approach, until he tapped him. Putting his hand over the receiver he whispered, "I'll be out in a minute."

Jackson spoke into the receiver and asked, "What time is best for you?" With a pause as to receive an answer, and then he responded, "Cool an hour is perfect."

Jackson hung up the phone, and began to explain, as he was approaching the door to check if it was locked the phone began to ring so he unlocked the door, and answered the phone.

"Tyrone you would have never guessed who it was."

"It was Brenda one of my old school honnies."

"I haven't seen, or heard from her for two years."

"She had gotten married on me," "Because I didn't want to commit and settle down, you feel me?"

"I can't have no broad telling what I can and can't do."

"That just aint me, you feel me?"

"But anyway, she just told me she missed me and wanted to see me."

"She'll be here in about an hour, she's flying in from Chicago."

Tyrone with a look of surprise, and disappointment said, "So what about all of us going out?"

Tyrone was thinking without Jackson, Tamika might not want to spend any time with him.

Then the loud roar of Tamika`s horn came blaring in to the house she was starting to get impatient.

Turning off the car, Tamika slid out of the driver's side and walked up to the front door.

Through the cracked door that Jackson and Tyrone left open, she could see the two men having a little pow wow, but she couldn`t quite make out the words that were being spoken.

She automatically got nosey, and tried to creep up close enough to ease drop. But as soon as she got close enough to hear Jackson was turning toward the front door to come outside.

Jackson was startled to see Tamika standing there.

"How long have you been standing there," asked Jackson?

"Not long enough, because I didn't get a chance to hear the conversation."

With a nervous look, Jackson smiled trying to read Tamika`s face to see if she was telling the truth.

"Since you're already out the car come on in."

Tyrone still standing there waiting for an answer to his question was starting to get impatient.

Trying to put the full court press on Jackson, Tyrone spoke up before Jackson could say anything and asked, "So what's up?"

Tyrone was thinking he might buckle under the pressure, and give in to keep their date.

Jackson in his mind began to think how he should word his thoughts.

Looking over at Tyrone Jackson said, "Yo bro you sure look good."

Then turning his attention to Tamika he said, "Baby you sure look fine."

"I was thinking that since both of you look so good apart."

"That together you two would look even better, you feel me?"

"You two walking into a club tonight will make everyone jealous."

"All the honnies will want you Tyrone,"

"Just think Tamika, he's all yours,"

"You won't have to share any of his attention with anyone else."

"You know Tamika all the fellows will be sweating you for some of your time, and conversation." "But she'll be all yours Tyrone."

"You'll be the envy of all the fellows tonight."

"So why don't you two remarkable people go to the club tonight without me."

"This will give both of you a chance to get to know one another."

"Without any added pressure from me, you feel me?"

Not giving them time to respond to his statement Jackson looking at Tyrone said, "Excuse me Tamika, can I please have a word with your date."

Jackson turned to head into the kitchen, while signaling Tyrone to follow him.

As they entered the kitchen Jackson leaned up against the counter top and folding his arms asked Tyrone, "So what do you think about Tamika?"

Tyrone began to smile and said, "Man she's everything you said she was, and then some, you feel me?"

"So you don't mind if I excuse myself and give you two love birds some personal time do you," asked Jackson?

Tyrone began to respond, "Jackson you know she doesn't really know me,"

"She might not want to go."

"If you're not coming with us, you feel me?"

Jackson could feel the anxiety from Tyrone's words.

He dropped his head to try to get his thoughts together. Slowly raising his head he said, "So how much do you really like her?"

Tyrone responded, "If I compare her to all the women I've ever dated."

"And I put all of my desires and qualifications into one woman."

"Then from what I've seen thus far," "She's everything I want in a women."

"I think she could be my wife."

Jackson unfolded his arms and put his hands in the air as to physically stop Tyrone's words.

Jackson said, "Woe cowboy slow your row."

"I was asking as far as to kick it with, you feel me?"

"Let's not put the cart before the horse."

"Look here if you keep being the perfect gentleman,"

"Then I don't think you'll have any problems."

"So take one step at a time," "Before you start talking like that."

"So with that said, here's a little something for you to woo her with."

Jackson dug deep into his pocket pulling out a bank roll that could choke a horse.

Licking his thumb he slowly peeled off four new fifty dollars bills and handed them to Tyrone.

"Now this should be enough to have a decent evening with, you feel me?"

Tyrone put the money in his pocket and he began to say, "This still doesn't change the fact that she doesn't know me, you feel me?"

Jackson put his hands on Tyrone's shoulders and turned him back toward the living room as a trainer leads his fighter into the ring, said, "Just do what we talked about and everything will be everything, you feel me?"

With all the apprehension of a prize fighter fighting his biggest fight.

He slowly allowed Jackson to lead him by his shoulders through the kitchen door.

Entering back into the living room, Tyrone put on the biggest smile he could muster, and turned to Tamika and said, "Since Jackson is being a lame."

"Why don`t me and you go party like a couple of rock stars?"

Tamika with a look of surprise from Tyrone`s question hesitated.

First looking at Tyrone and then looking past Tyrone at Jackson still not answering Tyrone`s question, stared at Jackson with a look of anger. Jackson sensing the anger staring into Tamika`s eyes once again silently formed the words.

"Please just try, and I`ll owe you one I promise."

Reading Jackson`s lips she began to smile and answered, "I would be honored to party like a rock star with you." Once again Tyrone extended his elbow to Tamika and, arm in arm they headed to the car.

Tyrone walked Tamika to the driver's side, and opened the car door for her. Making sure he was the perfect gentleman.

After closing the car door to walk back to the passenger's side, Tyrone behind the car he could see Tamika reach over to open his door. Tyrone was always told that if you open a door for a women and she doesn't reach over to open your door than that woman is a selfish woman.

Seeing that Tamika wasn`t being selfish brought a new found confidence to Tyrone.

Opening the door and getting inside Tyrone asked, "Where would you like to go?"

Tamika answered and said, "Since you're the man I'll go anywhere you want to take me."

Tyrone's confidence shot through the roof.

"Well I was thinking about the warehouse."

"Does that sound good to you?"

Before Tamika could answer Tyrone added, "You know they have jazz on the first floor and they serve dinner until 11:00."

Tamika glanced down at her watch, seeing it was only 9:30 said, "That should give us an hour and a half to order dinner."

Tyrone spoke up, "We did drink an awful lot of wine, and I would love to feed you." Tamika smiled and said "You're such a gentleman."

Smiling back Tyrone said, "I do what I can do, you feel me?" They both began to laugh as Tamika started the car.

.

Chapter Twelve

Pulling out of Jackson`s drive way Tyrone made a mental note to do something special for Jackson, to try and thank him for the hook up. As they drove down the street, out the corner of his eye Tyrone spotted Trouble and Bullethead pulled over on the side of the road by the police.

"Dam" he said out loud.

Startled by Tyrone`s comment she said, "What happened, did I do something wrong?"

Tyrone laughed and said, "No I just seen the two guys we were going to ride with tonight, pulled over by the police."

"I`m sure glad you weren`t with them" Tamika said,

"See how being with me is a blessing already."

Tyrone turned with a shocked expression and said, "I feel you baby."

Then Tamika added, "I`m an angel sent from heaven, just for you." Very confused and excited Tyrone looking at Tamika could only smile.

Because he truly did think she was an angel sent from heaven.

Tyrone decided to lean back and enjoy the ride to the warehouse without a lot of conversation. He didn`t want to put his foot in his mouth to early.

Tyrone didn`t have a lot of experience with beautiful women, and he really didn`t know what to say. Tyrone reached down turning up the radio allowing the music to break the silence in the car so they both could relax.

A short time later as they pulled into the warehouse parking lot Tamika commented that the line to go into the club was extremely long. She looked over at Tyrone she said, "Do you still want to go in?" Tyrone looked back and said, "Yes."

Riding through the parking lot Tamika found a spot and slowly pulled the caddy in and parked.

She turned off the car, and as she sat there, she said, "Do you really want to go stand in that long line?" Tyrone smiled and said, "I know it`s kind of chilly and you don`t have on a jacket,"

"So I understand your apprehension."

Tamika interrupted, and added, "And I don't have on anything on under this dress."

"I don't like wearing panties."

Shocked and excited Tyrone couldn't respond.

Tamika took it upon herself to say it again.

"Did you hear me Tyrone?" "I said I don't have on any panties!"

Tyrone cleared the frog from his throat and said, "Yes I heard you."

"I was just surprised hearing you say that."

"But don't worry we won't have to wait in line very long," said Tyrone.

"Why not," asked Tamika?

"Don't worry I'll handle it, "said Tyrone.

"Ok" Tamika said reluctantly.

"Just remember you don't want my pussy to get cold, you feel me?"

"Oh I feel you baby,"

"We definitely don't want that to happen."

As they walked up to the long line, Tyrone took off his jacket and slid it around Tamika's shoulders trying to prevent her from getting cold.

Tyrone looking up to the front of the line said, "Excuse me for a second Tamika,"

"I'll be right back."

Walking past all the cold people standing in line Tyrone spotted a friend he went to school with working the door. Walking up with his hand extended to shake his friends hand.

Tyrone hollered, "Yo bro what`s been happening?"

As the guy looked up to see who was speaking to him he began to smile. Grabbing Tyrone`s hand pulling him in to hug him said, "What`s been up bro" sliding his tree trunk arms around Tyrone.

Tyrone hugging the brother said, "You know the same old, same old."

Tyrone had known Gus since high school when they played football together, and over the years they became pretty good friends.

Tyrone said, "Hey Gus I need a favor."

"I got the coldest women I`ve ever been out with."

"I was wondering if you can let us cut to the front of the line tonight."

Gus began to smile and said, "For you bro anything."

Tyrone gave Gus another hug and said, "Cool I`ll go get her and be right back."

Walking back to Tamika Tyrone could only smile.

Slightly starting to shiver, Tamika looked at Tyrone with a look of anger and said, "I thought you forgot about me."

"You left me standing here in the cold,"

"Now my pussy is cold."

As Tamika was turning to leave Tyrone grabbed Tamika by the hand, and looking into her eyes said in a low sweet voice, "Wow baby I`m sorry."

"I didn`t mean to be gone so long."

"And if your pussy got cold."

"Maybe I need to blow some of my hot breath on it,"

"To warm it back up."

Tamika commented, "I just might have to take you up on that offer before the night is over." They both laughed as Tyrone put his arms around Tamika`s shoulders and they headed for the front of the line.

Chapter Thirteen

Once they reached the front of the line Tyrone introduced Tamika to Gus. Gus extended his massive hand and said, "It`s a pleasure to meet you."

Tamika shook his hand and said, "Like wise."

Tyrone spoke up and said, "My main man here is looking out for us tonight."

"I told him that you were too beautiful to be standing in the cold."

Gus interrupted and said, "She sure is."

"So why don`t two lovely people come on in and enjoy your evening."

Giving Tyrone five, Gus removed the red velvet rope allowing them to come in.

Inside Tyrone led Tamika by the hand down the hall of men standing by the entrance all hoping to snag a lovely young woman coming in alone. All the guys seeing Tamika and Tyrone together could only stare in amazement.

Tamika`s nipples were still hard from her standing out in the cold, and with the very thin dress she wore her perfect size breast with hard nipples were eye candy.

A huge smile formed on Tyrone`s face seeing all the jealous guys stare and start to point.

While they strolled past the hallway of predators Tamika noticed all the ladies staring at Tyrone, as he held her hand. The fact of them being jealous made her feel like a queen walking with her king.

Simultaneously the words Jackson had spoken to them at his house entered into their minds, and they both turned to each other and said, "Are you thinking what I`m thinking?"

They both at the same time said, "That Jackson is something else." Tamika and Tyrone both laughed and gave each other a hug.

Smiling, Tyrone said, "I`m glad we both have a friend like Jackson."

"Me to," said Tamika "Now let's find a table so we can eat,"

"Because I`m starving," "If you don`t feed me soon," "I might eat you."

Tamika grabbed Tyrone by the hand and began to playfully nibble on his finger.

Taking Tyrone's finger out of her mouth but still holding his hand Tamika led Tyrone to a small cozy table in the corner, overlooking the waterfront.

The ambiance in the room was breath taking every table had a fine white linen table cloth with lace around the outside edges along with white candles sitting in a fourteen karat gold candle holder.

There was also a single white rose in a Waterford crystal vase.

The only light in the room came from the candles that burned on each table.

Tamika asked Tyrone, "Is this alright?"

Tyrone could only smile seeing Tamika pick the most romantic table she could find.

Tyrone walked over to Tamika, and acting like she was royalty, pulled out her chair, and slowly grabbed her hand to make sure she was seated comfortably.

Not releasing her once she was seated Tyrone bent down and gently kissed her hand.

Tyrone rose from his bent over position, and asked Tamika if she needed anything before he sat down?

Standing in the candle light Tamika looked at Tyrone like he was her tall dark prince charming that stepped off the pages of a fairy tale novel.

She felt at that moment like she was Cinderella and all her wishes were coming true.

As Tyrone turned to walk over to his chair Tamika could only stare at Tyrone's ass wondering how it would feel to pull his ass down in between her long muscular thighs.

Tyrone sat down and only stared at Tamika he didn't know what to say he had never dated a woman so beautiful. Her green eyes seemed to glow in the dim light piercing his very soul. Tyrone stunned that he was on a date with such a goddess was bewildered. His mind went blank and he could only be thankful they were together.

But before things could get awkward the waiter brought them the fanciest, gold embossed, menus they both had ever seen.

Opening the menus Tyrone took it upon his self to order for them both.

"He told the waiter bring us a bottle of Merlo,"

"And some oysters on the half shell for appetizers."

"Then we`ll have main lobster, and prime rib for our entrée's."

Closing the menu Tyrone stuck out his chest because he was glad he had taken charge. It was his first time he had ever ordered food, without checking the prices first.

Tyrone reached over and grabbed Tamika`s hand and said, "Thank you, for the best date I`ve ever been on." Then he added, "I mean that with all my heart."

Tamika looked honored to hear such a compliment and said, "Your very welcome sir."

"But why are you making it seemed like this is the end of the date."

"That`s something you say at the end of the date."

"This is only the beginning," she said with a devilish smile.

The waiter returned with the wine, and the oysters sitting on crushed ice.

The silver platter the oysters sat on sparkled under the candle light.

As the waiter left Tyrone looked over at Tamika and said, "Can I be honest with you?"

Tamika with a puzzled look said, "Yes."

Tyrone started to smile and said, "I have a confession to make," "I've never eaten oysters before."

"I just thought it sounded cool to order."

Tamika looked at Tyrone and said, "Me neither."

"I thought it was something you liked."

Tyrone and Tamika both began to laugh, now that the ice was finally broken.

Tamika used her napkin to dry the tears from her eyes from laughing so hard. Staring at the oysters Tamika said, "Tyrone if you'll try one, then I'll try one."

Tyrone looked at Tamika and said, "Since this is the first time for both of us,"

"Let's try them together."

Coming together in agreement, they both reached over to grab an oyster.

Tyrone looked at Tamika and said, "I don't think I can do this."

Looking down at the slime covered oyster. Tyrone asked, "Is there something you're supposed to put on it to help the taste?"

Tamika looked on the platter and said, "There's some horse radish sauce",

"I guess you use that to help the taste."

Tyrone grabbed the horse radish sauce, and began to cover the entire oyster.

Tamika commented, "I think you might have put too much on there,"

"Horse radish sauce is kind of hot."

Tyrone ignoring Tamika's comment said, "On three." They reached over and touched oysters and Tyrone began to count, "One, two, and three."

On three they both opened wide and completely engulfed their oysters.

Tyrone immediately reached for the wine, pouring, and gulping down an entire glass.

After swallowing the wine Tyrone took a deep breath and said, "You weren't lying that horse radish sauce aint no joke."

Tamika began to laugh and said, "I'm sorry."

"I didn't mean to laugh, are you alright?"

Letting out a deep sigh of relieve. Tyrone said, "Yeah, I'm fine."

Regaining his composure he said, "That wasn't half bad." Tamika commented, "Mine really didn't have any taste to it."

"It was just slimy."

Tyrone added, "I also heard that oysters are good for your sex drive."

Tamika said with a smile, "I heard that to."

"So since they weren't half bad,"

"Then eat up, because I think you might need your strength for later."

Tyrone looked up and half-heartedly laughed.

Because he really didn't know what Tamika was saying but he was afraid to ask her to clarify her statement.

Tyrone grabbed another oyster and said, "Down the hatch," turning his head toward the sky, and then swallowing the next few like an old pro.

Tamika said, "It looks like you finally got the hang of it." Finishing the platter of oysters .Tyrone poured them both a glass of wine and said, "I would like to toast to prosperity," "And a long lasting beautiful friendship."

Tamika said, "I would like to add here's to fairy tales coming true."

With a look of bewilderment, Tyrone touched glasses and took a nice sip of wine.

As they were putting down their glasses, the waiter wheeled a cart next to their table, bringing their entrées. Tyrone looked up and said, "They sure have good service here."

The waiter hearing Tyrone's comment said," Only the best for the best."

"Is this a special occasion tonight" "Maybe a wedding anniversary perhaps?"

Tyrone looked surprised the waiter thought they were together as a couple. Before Tyrone could answer, Tamika spoke up and said, "Yes."

"This is our one year anniversary." The waiter smiled and said, "Still newlyweds how sweet after your meal I`ll bring you two a complimentary dessert."

Tyrone looking at Tamika with a surprised look said, "Thank you we sure do appreciate that."

The waiter finished serving them dinner and as he rolled the cart away Tyrone asked Tamika, "Why did you tell him that?"

Tamika smiled and said, "It gave us something to celebrate, "We did get a free dessert."

"Who knows it might just come true for next year."

"This could be our table, and our special meal we order on our wedding anniversary." "Wedding anniversary?" Tyrone began to choke.

Tamika looked up from her food and stared Tyrone right in the eyes and said, "You heard me, I said wedding anniversary." "I think we would make a nice couple don`t you agree?"

Tyrone had the warmest feeling he had ever felt in his entire life if he died right then and there he would die the happiest man on earth.

After hearing Tamika`s question Tyrone said "Yes we would," "I would be honored to be your husband," and began to eat his food, and only occasionally glanced up to smile at Tamika.

Tyrone was afraid to talk, he didn`t want to change Tamika`s mind or mess up the moment by saying something stupid. He never had a woman make those type of comments to him before, he was in foreign territory and wasn't quite sure how to approach the situation. Being quiet was his only option.

After they were done eating Tamika spoke first, "That was a delicious meal."

"Wouldn't you agree Tyrone?"

Tyrone grabbing his glass in full agreement raised it and said, "Yes it was," "A perfect meal, on a perfect evening, on a perfect date."

The waiter after seeing them finishing their meal, brought over the dessert cart, and asked them to pick which one they wanted to eat.

Tamika said, "I really shouldn't I have to watch my figure."

Tyrone spoke up and said, "You don't have to watch it."

"I'll watch it for you sweetheart." The waiter and Tamika both chuckled.

Then the waiter added, "Can I suggest a low fat piece of cheese cake."

Tyrone said, "Since this is our anniversary we might as well go all out."

"Please give us the triple chocolate fudge cake with chocolate ice cream."

The waiter said, "That is an excellent choice."

"I'll bring that right out to you."

As soon as the waiter left Tamika said, "I can't eat that," rubbing her hands down her stomach and thighs insinuating where the pounds would accumulate after she ate the dessert.

Tyrone jokingly said, "This is our anniversary, you feel me?" They both laughed as they waited for their dessert.

Tyrone sitting there waiting for the dessert to come could only wonder how Jackson`s evening was turning out. Pondering about Jackson`s evening Tyrone said, "I know you and Jackson are friends, and I don`t want to be too forward."

"But do you think I can see you again?" Tamika just laughed.

"There you go again acting like this date is over." Leaning forward in her chair and reaching over to touch Tyron`s hand she said, "This has been the best date of my life."

"So why would I not want to see you again?"

"Yeah your right, me and Jackson are friends",

"That`s the key word friends."

Letting go of Tyrone`s hands and sitting back in her chair she said, "I hope it won`t bother you that me and Jackson were intimate."

"I don`t want that to keep us from getting to know each other."

Tyrone had never thought about that before.

He asked himself if he could handle the fact that Jackson and Tamika had been intimate. Pausing before he answered Tamika`s question.

Tyrone said, "Tamika you weren`t a virgin when you met Jackson were you? "She shook her head no answering Tyrone`s question.

"So he wasn`t your first" "Then if I get mad about you and him being together."

"I would have to get mad about every guy you`ve ever been with, you feel me?"

"Jackson is my friend." "He`s closer to me than a brother."

"No it won`t bother me a bit,"

"Because I`m thinking about the good times we can have together, you feel me?"

"But thanks for asking."

Once the dessert came they shared it, and talked about their past relationships.

Feeling like he had gotten to know her a little better. Tyrone suggested they leave the dining room, and go dance off some of the food they had just eaten.

As the waiter was bringing the check Tyrone reached in his pocket and pulled out his money. He had already calculated the bill in his head so adding in a nice tip he counted out one hundred dollars, and placed the money on the table.

Then he walked over to Tamika and kindly pulled her chair out from the table.

Gently grabbing her by the hand Tyrone escorted Tamika to the bar where they were playing some nice smooth jazz. Tyrone still holding Tamika`s hand said, "Can I please have this dance?"

Tamika looked Tyrone in his eyes and said, "I would be honored."

Walking over to the dance floor they begun to dance and became lost in each other's arms.

Tamika and Tyrone both became oblivious to their surroundings.

Tamika could only hold Tyrone and wonder why she had been so hesitant before she felt so safe in his arms she didn't want the song to end.

Tyrone had been the perfect gentleman all night he never talked about sex or talked about how good he was in bed. She was surprised how much she wanted to open up to him.

Tamika took her head off Tyrone's shoulder for a second and whispered in his ear "Please don't ever let me go."

Tyrone hearing those words gently squeezed her in his arms and said, "I won't I promise."

Close to the end of the song Tyrone walked Tamika over to the bar and said, "Excuse me for a minute I have to use the restroom."

Tyrone looked at Tamika and said, "Can I trust you around all of these guys in here?"

Smiling, Tamika said, "Baby you don't have anything to worry about."

"I'll be here when you get back I promise."

Smiling from ear to ear Tyrone went to the restroom, and on his way out from the john he stopped to use his phone to call Jackson.

Tyrone dug deep in his pocket past the money for his cell phone.

Finding his I phone he began dialing Jackson's number. Waiting for Jackson to answer, Tyrone could only smile. The phone rang a few times, and then Tyrone heard Jackson answer.

Jackson said, "Hello."

Tyrone responded, "Yo bro what's going on?"

Jackson began to laugh and said, "Nothing much, how`s your date going?"

Tyrone lit up like a Christmas tree at the question Jackson asked him and said, "Jackson I just couldn`t wait to tell you how good the date is going."

"I just wanted to say thank you for the best date in my whole life."

Tyrone said, "I owe you so much."

"I`ll do whatever I can do for you,"

"I don`t care what it is. I`ll do it, you feel me?"

"Wash your car cut the grass whatever you need bro I got you."

Before Jackson could respond Tyrone said, "I just wanted to let you know how good it`s going."

"I don`t want to keep her waiting too long,"

"I`ll holler at you later, "Tyrone hung up the phone and turned the power off so no one could interrupt his magical date.

Jackson hearing how excited Tyrone was filled him with a warm, fuzzy feeling all over.

Hanging up the phone, Jackson walked back into his living room, and poured himself another glass of wine.

Eagerly awaiting his date to arrive Jackson decided to set the mood he put on his best slow jam cd, and dimmed the lights to set the ambiance.

Sipping on his glass of wine the phone rang again. Jackson thought it was Tyrone calling back and he answered, "What`s up bro?"

The voice that came back to him said, "Can I speak to Jackson?"

Jackson quickly got himself together and said, "Excuse me, I thought you were someone else."

The woman's voice on the other end sounded sexy, and was full of excitement.

She quickly said, "Hey baby this is Brenda, are you busy?"

Jackson responded, "No baby I was just waiting for you to get here."

"Ok that's great because I'll be there in about twenty minutes."

"I'm here at the airport and I'm just waiting for my rental car to pull up"

"I've missed you so much."

"I have a wonderful surprise for you."

Jackson interrupted and said, "You're all the surprise I need baby."

Brenda interrupted and said, "I see my car pulling up, I'll be there in a minute, see you soon," hanging up the phone.

Jackson hung up the phone, and walked from room to room making sure everything was in its proper place. After inspecting the house he walked over to the hallway mirror to do another inspection of himself.

After the inspection and being satisfied at what he saw. He sat down on the couch and began to sip his wine again.

After listening to a couple of songs on his favorite cd the doorbell rang. Jackson slowly got up to answer the door.

As he turned the lock to open the door he slightly cracked the door, then suddenly the door burst open and before he could react Brenda was all over him hugging and kissing him.

After Jackson realized it was only Brenda and not a home invasion.

He relaxed and said, "Woe baby, pushing her arms from around him."

He said, "Baby you kind of startled me a little." Brenda with a smile bright enough to lighten up the darkest day, said "I`m sorry baby I didn`t mean to startle you."

"I was just so excited I couldn`t help myself."

Jackson took a step back and said, "Let me have a good look at you." Brenda turned slowly showing all of her beauty.

Brenda asked, "Do I still look the same?"

Jackson paused for a minute and said "No."

Brenda quickly responded, "What do you mean no." While she rubbed her hands across her flat stomach and took her hands under her voluptuous breast raising them to Jackson`s attention. Releasing them and rubbing her hands down her body down to her tapered waist and firm but tender backside.

"I don`t turn you on anymore?"

Jackson said, "You didn`t give me a chance to finish what I was saying."

"You look more stunning than I remember."

"When I look at you now," "Your beauty is breath taking."

Brenda was five foot four with amber eyes she weighed 125 lbs. and her measurements were 34d and 24inch waist with 32inch hips.

Her skin was so soft it didn't feel real, it felt like a mixture of babies skin with 1000 thread count Egyptian cotton.

It was so amazingly soft you had to wonder if you were dreaming.

For her to be so beautiful she wasn't vain she was completely down to earth.

Brenda showed up wearing a sequence dress and matching shoes she had a small amount of glitter on her arms and chest. From her head to her toes the light made the sequence in her dress and shoes along with glitter on her arms and chest shine like she was cover in diamonds. The lip-gloss she wore made her lips so seductive and sensual.

She smelled so good that her perfume was intoxicating.

Brenda walked up to Jackson, and began to kiss him passionately. She slowly slid her tongue in and out of his mouth and she took one hand and began to massage his chest, and with her other hand she began to stroke his dick causing Jackson to get an erection.

Standing there with a full hard on, Jackson grabbed her hands and eased out of her grip, and said, "Slow down baby we got all night for that lets sit down for a minute."

Brenda caught off guard by Jackson's comment backed up, she had never had a man tell her to stop so she was surprised.

Staring at Jackson she said, "I'm sorry baby it's been a while and I've missed you so much you have no idea."

Jackson said, "Let me go and get your bags from the car then we can talk."

Once Jackson went to the car to retrieve her bags they sat on the couch and began to catch up.

Jackson said, "So tell me about Chicago."

Brenda`s eyes lit up "Chicago is so wonderful, you would love it there."

"My husband and I have a mansion right outside the city."

Jackson interrupted and said, "So you're still married?"

Brenda dropped her head and said, "Yes."

Jackson asked her, "So why are you here?"

"My husband is a very important business man and he`s always gone."

"He leaves me home alone for months at a time."

"I haven`t seen him for the last two months so I decided if he can leave so can I."

"I called you and you said you were available so whala her I am."

"I`m comfortable financially but I`m extremely lonely"

Jackson could see the hurt in her eyes, and asked, "Have you talked to him about this?"

Brenda said, "I`ve tried to talk to him several times, but he doesn't listen to me."

"I think he just wants me as a trophy"

"For business meetings and for public events,"

"He wants everyone to see a beautiful woman on his arm other than that I`m always home alone. "I feel like all the time and effort I put into my education to obtain my degrees was a waste of time." "I`m still being controlled by a man, my sole purpose for going to school was to be independent and self-sufficient."   She began to break down and cry.

Jackson grabbed her and held her in his arms as tight as he could.

He whispered, "Don`t worry baby it`s going to be alright."

Regaining her composure Brenda said, "I`m sorry I didn`t mean to break down in front of you."

"But I haven't had anyone to hold me in so long."

"When I kissed you I lost control."

Then with a devilish smirk she added, "You always were and still is the best I`ve ever had."

"I love your dick I've never stopped thinking about you."

Ignoring her last statement Jackson looked at Brenda and said, "It`s a shame that your husband doesn't realize the precious gift he`s been given."

"But anyway, it is really good to see you."

"Would you like a glass of wine?"

Brenda said, "I would love one thank you. "Brenda taking the glass of wine from Jackson`s hand began to plot how she was going to have sex with him.

They sat back on the couch and talked and drank, and before they realized it the whole bottle was gone.

While sipping her wine Brenda had allowed her mind to take her on a stroll down memory lane. She pictured Jackson dick sliding in and out her pussy and she was getting turned on.

Trying to refocusing on the present and with a smile she said, "It's a little warm in here do you mind if I relax a little more." Jackson looked at her and said, "My home is your home."

"It's not a mansion but you're welcome to come whenever you would like to visit."

Brenda looked Jackson in his eyes and said, "I want to cum right now."

Brenda turned around and said, "Please unzip my dress." Jackson slowly unzipped her dress exposing her baby soft skin.

Once unzipped, Brenda stood up and allowed the dress to fall to her ankles. She stepped out of the dress leaving it lay where it fell.

Brenda grabbed Jackson by the hand and pulled him to his feet. Once Jackson was standing he admired her beauty like he was a deer caught in headlights, he was star struck. He had forgotten how beautiful she was.

She wore a black lace bra and matching lace thongs. Brenda asked Jackson to undress, so he did and stood there completely naked.

After he was naked she got on her knees she wanted to taste his dick in her mouth. Jackson watched as her mouth slowly engulfed his dick until the blood rushing into his dick made it throb and swell in her mouth.

While she pleasured Jackson she pulled her lace panties to the side so she could massage her clitoris. She rubbed herself violently getting her pussy hot and wet so Jackson's dick could enter her.

Hot and wet Brenda sat Jackson back down on the couch so she could straddle him. She pushed his legs together and propped his dick straight up making it easy for her small frame to mount such a big dick.

Turning her body facing away from him she reached down between her legs and placed Jackson's brick hard dick up to her outer lips. She began to rub his rock hard dick up against her lips wetting the head of his dick.

Moaning from the rock hard dick touching her pussy Brenda said, "I can't wait to give you this pussy."

It had been so long since she was able to feel like a woman she didn't even take off her panties.

She just pulled them to the side, and began to easy down then raising back up to the very tip of his manhood. With every descent she wet up his dick more and more making sure he went a little deeper every time.

Jackson with only half of his dick inside watched as she tightened up like her whole body was instantly frozen and she began to have an orgasm.

The wetness oozed down his dick onto his balls and thighs, she was truly backed up and now she had an opportunity to release she was going to take full advantage of the situation.

After the initial orgasm Brenda placed her hands on her thighs and braced herself for the Hugh dick to enter her.

She pushed down hard forcing his dick deeper inside. She felt like his dick was traveling up through her body.

She closed her eyes and held her breath until his entire dick was inside of her leaving only his balls visible.

Jackson seeing her pussy engulf his dick got excited and placed his hands around her small waist and raised her body up just enough so he could be in control.

First he started with slow even strokes giving her pussy a good gentle fucking.

Moving his dick in and out making her moan louder and louder gave Jackson motivation to continue on his mission. Goosh goosh goosh the sound her pussy made told Jackson he was doing a good job of fulfilling her passion. Brenda went limp in his arms from the exquisite attention her pussy was receiving.

She felt like she was being control by the dick Jackson wielded, it was like she was under a hypnotic spell cast by his dick.

Jackson feeling her body go limp in his arms began to pond her pussy fast and hard, the gentleness was gone now he wanted to fuck her into submission.

Jackson's stroke was so hard every time he entered her his balls smacked her clitoris giving her added pleasure.

Tightening his grip to control her, he slowed down and began delivering smooth strokes once again, only he pulled his dick out all the way barely leavening the head still inside then slowly driving his entire dick back inside. He continued his stroke until he felt like he was about to explode. Not wanting to cum Jackson took his dick out of her and waited for a few seconds before reentering her.

Once back inside he resumed the pounding of her pussy, Jackson told Brenda to play with her nipples while he pounded her tight little twat.

Once she began to touch herself she began to cum all over Jackson's dick. As Brenda came she said, "Please give me a baby," "Please cum inside my pussy."

Brenda sat down hard on Jackson's dick and began to thrust her hips violently, trying to make Jackson come inside of her.

Jackson could no longer stand it he began to cum trying to push her off his dick. But Brenda was determined to receive every last drop of cum he had to offer and she spread her legs open wide and sat down ready to receive all he had to offer. Jackson exploded deep inside her letting out grunts of pleasure as he filled her up with cum. Now that Brenda had gotten what she wanted.

She unsaddled Jackson and lay on the floor with her legs elevated in the air.

Jackson leaned back on the couch still bothered by what had just happened, asked, "What was that all about?"

Brenda still lying on her back with her legs in the air said, "I want a baby,"

"Either my husband can`t have children or he won`t give me one."

"But it doesn't matter now."

Jackson still bothered said, "So what are you going to tell him when you have this baby and it doesn't look like him?"

"He`ll probably divorce me and put me out" said Brenda.

Jackson was really confused now, "Look here Brenda" Jackson stated.

"I`m not ready to take care of a child,"

"I don`t want to be forced into settling down."

"Don`t worry Jackson."

"I don`t want anything from you."

"I actually brought you something"

"This is the surprise I wanted to give you."

Brenda finally got up from off her back and retrieved her purse. Reaching in her purse she pulled out a check and handed it to Jackson.

Jackson opened the check and read the amount it read five hundred thousand dollars. Jackson rubbed his eyes as if he had read the amount incorrectly "Brenda what `s going on, "asked Jackson?

Casually Brenda began to get dressed, Ignoring Jackson`s question.

She put on her clothes and while kissing Jackson on the cheek she said, "Thank you baby." Jackson wasn`t satisfied with her nonchalant attitude standing up to confront Brenda Jackson grabbed Brenda by her arm and said, "I need an explanation."

"You walk in here and fuck my brains out and tell me to impregnate you,"

"Then you hand me a check for five hundred thousand dollars."

"I need some answers, you feel me?"

Brenda just casually grinned and said, "I`ll explain it to you, if you just let go of my arm and calm down."

Jackson released her arm and sat back down on the couch. Brenda sat down beside Jackson after she slipped on her shoes.

She began to explain that her husband was very rich, and he had already given he over ten million dollars. So if he left her today it really didn't matter. The only missing piece to the puzzle is a baby. I'll use the money to start a business and care for my child by myself. Jackson asked, "So why are you giving me this money?"

"Because you're the only guy I've really ever loved,"

"I just wanted to show you just how much I love you."

Brenda leaned over and kissed Jackson on the forehead and said, "Well I think I'd better be going now."

Breda picked up her bags and walked to the front door.

Pausing before she left she turned and blew Jackson a kiss and said, "You know if I'm not pregnant I'm coming back until you get it right."

Brenda opened the door and laughed all the way to her car.

Jackson was so surprised he couldn't believe what had just happened even for him this was very unusual.

Jackson sitting on the couch still naked decided well, "It's still early so I might as well go kick it." Picking up his clothes and the check he headed up the steps making a bee line for his bedroom. Jackson still holding the check in his hand smiled and placed it on the night stand beside the bed.

Quickly jumping in the shower he got dressed and walked to his garage. He hadn't wanted to drive, but now he really didn't have a choice.

Opening his garage Jackson pulled out the sparkling clean Mercedes. Jackson paused just to make sure he hadn't forgotten anything. He went through his mental check list.

"I got my house keys"

"I got money,"

"I got my driver's license," upon completing his inspection he closed the garage and headed toward his destination.

While driving Jackson noticed his gas hand was low so he headed to the nearest gas station to fill up.

Once he reached the gas station he swiped his credit card and began to pump the gas, and out the corner of his eye he spotted Trouble and Bullethead walking up toward him.

"Yo Jackson what's up", Trouble asked?

Jackson turned to face Trouble and said, "Nothing what's up with you?"

Trouble asked, "So where you headed?"

"Why", asked Jackson?

Bullethead spoke up and said, "Because we figured if you were going to kick it, then we wanted to ride with you."

Jackson laughed and said, "Like me and Tyrone wanted to kick it with you and Trouble,"

"You rolled out on us right."

"Now you want a ride." Trouble and Bullethead were speechless for a second and said, "My bag I owe you one, you feel me?" Jackson looking at Trouble and Bullethead asked, "Where's your car Trouble?"

Trouble started to laugh. "The police impounded my shit earlier,"

"They said I had some unpaid parking tickets."

Jackson said, "Well I'm headed to the warehouse you and Bullethead can ride if you want."

Bullethead said, "Yo Trouble we aint dressed for that."

"But the impound station isn't far from there."

"Let's ride over to the warehouse with Jackson from there we can walk to pick up the car, you feel me?"

Trouble looked at Jackson and said. "Do you think I could borrow a couple of dollars?"

Jackson looked at Trouble and asked, "How much is a couple?" Trouble dug into his pocket and pulled out three crumpled ten dollar bills and said, "I need seventy dollars if you can spare it."

Jackson paused and said, "No problem,"

"You and Bullethead can borrow the money after I go pay for the gas."

Trouble and Bullethead got in while Jackson went into the gas station. Jackson didn't have to go inside because he had used his credit card to pay for the gas. Jackson didn't want to pull out his money in front of Trouble and Bullethead.

Entering the service station Jackson asked the clerk, "Where do you keep the gum?" The clerk pointed over to the far isle and said, "It should be on the top shelf in between the candy bars and the breath mints."

Jackson walked over to the far isle out of site from everyone and pulled out his money and counted out seventy one dollars. With money in hand he headed over to the counter to pay for the gum.

As Jackson stood in the line the guy in front of him was acting very nervous. Finally all the people paid for their gas and there was only Jackson and the nervous guy that was in line before him.

The guy reached into his pocket and pulled out a gun and ordered the clerk to empty out the register.

Jackson was so shocked, he couldn't believe he was in the middle of an armed robbery Jackson thought this is shit you only see on TV. The clerk opened the drawer and handed the robber all the cash in the register.

Receiving the money from the clerk the robber turned the gun on Jackson and ordered him to give him the money he held in his hand. In Jackson's mind he was thinking what's going to happen next.

The robber having grabbed the money from Jackson's hand and the money from the clerk quickly fled the gas station.

As soon as the robber left the clerk called the police Jackson still stunned couldn't believe what had just happened.

He walked out to his car and told Trouble and Bullethead what just took place Trouble and Bullethead began to laugh.

Jackson asked, "What's so funny I was just involved in an armed robbery." Trouble said,

"Me and Bullethead were going to rob the gas station if you weren't going to give us the money."

"But since you were going to let us borrow the money we decided not to"

Jackson dug into his pocket and counted out another seventy dollars and handed it to Trouble.

Jackson at this point didn`t care if they see how much money he had in his pocket. Jackson handed trouble the money and told them to get out of the car.

"I`m not headed in that direction,"

"You and Bullethead need to find another way to the impound station."

Trouble and Bullethead got out of the car and Jackson headed back into the gas station. He wrote down his name and address and told the clerk he wasn`t going to wait for the police.

He walked to his car and drove away as Jackson was driving down the street headed back to his house he glanced down at the radio displaying the time.

The time read 12:00am Jackson thought how hard it had been trying to go out all the things he had faced just to go out seemed ridiculous.

Then a feeling of anger came over him, and in his mind he was determined to keep his plans. Turning his car around Jackson headed for the expressway.

While on the expressway Jackson swore to himself come hell or high water he was going out. Quickly reaching his exit he headed for the warehouse.

Once he parked his car Jackson sat there for a minute to regain his composure. He slid out the car and headed up to the long awaiting line.

Jackson knew he didn`t have to stand in the cold, because he had VIP status. As he walked past all the people in line someone reached out and grabbed him by the arm and started to hug him.

Pulling away Jackson wanted to see who was putting their arms around him. As he stepped back Jackson seen it was one of his high school sweethearts.

Jackson smiled and said, "How you are?"

"I haven't seen you since we graduated." Shirley was the head cheerleader back in high school. She was built like a coke bottle with strong muscular legs that were very limber. She was voted most likely to succeed because she always got good grades.

Jackson grabbed Shirley by the hand and asked, "Who are you with?" Hoping she didn't name a male.

Shirley pointed to the girl that stood in line with her. Shirley took the girl by her hand and said, "This is Jackson my high school sweetheart."

"Jackson this is my girlfriend Debbie." Debbie extended her hand to shake Jackson's hand.

Shaking Debbie's hand Jackson paused for a second and asked, "Do you two lovely ladies want to party with me tonight?"

Shirley and Debbie quickly jumped out of line and they both grabbed one of Jackson's hands leading them both up to the front of the line.

Reaching the entrance Gus spoke up, "How are you doing this evening Mr. Jackson?"

As he eye balled the two women that stood on both sides of Jackson, Jackson started to laugh because Gus had addressed him as Mr. Jackson.

"I'm fine sir how are you doing tonight," asked Jackson?

Gus looked at the two women that were with Jackson and said, "If I had what you have I'd be doing a whole lot better." They all laughed and Gus removed the velvet rope and let them in.

As Jackson and his dates passed by, Gus leaned over and at a whisper asked Jackson, "How do you do it," "I just want to know your secret?"

Jackson laughed and gave Gus five as he escorted his dates into the bar.

Reaching the bar Jackson got the attention of the bar maid and said, "Bring us a bottle of champagne over to that corner table." Pointing to a secluded table he always sat at whenever he visited there.

Jackson making his way over to the table to sit down saw Tyrone and Tamika out on the dance floor slow dancing. Jackson smiled and asked Shirley and Debbie "Do you two want to dance?" Confused for a moment Shirley spoke up and said, "This is a slow song."

"How are you going to dance with both of us at the same time?"

Debbie added, "Yeah tell us how you're going to do it I want to hear this one."

Jackson just smiled and said, "Don't worry ladies, let's dance." They all walked onto the dance floor and Jackson put one in front of him and the other one he stood behind him.

Jackson put his hands in the air and turned from woman to woman. At first he faced Shirley, rubbing her body Jackson softly kissed her lips.

Then turning his back on Shirley, giving his attention to Debbie, all the while Shirley kept dancing grinding on Jackson's back allowing Debbie and Jackson to kiss.

Shirley put her arms around Jackson's waist and slow danced with his back. Turning once again to face Shirley he asked, "Didn't I ask you to trust me? "

Putting his arms in the air he slowly put an arm around Shirley's waist and the other arm he put around Debbie's waist and they all danced until the song started to end.

Tyrone spotted the canary yellow suit out of the corner of his eye. Tapping Tamika to get her attention she slowly opened her eyes because she had closed her eyes allowing the music to carry her away.

She felt so safe in Tyrone's arms she was unaware to her surroundings. Tyrone pointed to where Jackson and his dates were and said, "Do you want to join them."

Tamika said, "I'm having such a wonderful evening with you I don't want to share your attention with anyone tonight."

Tyrone said, "Let's at least go and speak." Reluctantly she agreed. Tyrone holding Tamika's hand walked over to Jackson.

Jackson put his arms around both women and stood in his Mack daddy pose as Tyrone and Tamika walked up to them.

Jackson reached out and hugged Tyrone and said, "It's good to see ya bro." Releasing Tyrone He began to introduce his dates to Tyrone.

Taking his hand and placing them around their waist once again as he introduced them, this is Shirley and this is Debbie. Tyrone smiling at Jackson looked at each women and said "It's nice to meet you." Tyrone already knew Shirley, but eyeballed Debbie like she was candy for his sweet tooth.

Tyrone was being cordial because he was with Tamika. Pulling Tamika in front of him placing his arms around her hips he said, "This is my beautiful friend Tamika."

Tamika shook both women hands and turned to hug Tyrone.

Jackson said, "I see you love birds hit it off pretty good."

"I would ask you two to join us but I can see you`ve been doing pretty good without me." Jackson asked Tyrone, "Where are you sitting?"

Tyrone pointed to the opposite corner and said, "We were sitting over there."

Jackson asked, "Do you mind if I buy you and Tamika something to drink."

Tyrone looked at Tamika to get her response, she just shrugged her shoulders and said, "I don`t care."

"Fine" said Jackson, "I`ll send it over through the bar maid."

Shaking Tyrone`s hand they parted ways and went back to their opposite tables.

Going back to the table the bar maid was just bringing the champagne he ordered.

As the bar maid placed the champagne on ice Jackson asked, "Can you please take another bottle of champagne to the table in the opposite corner where Tyrone and Tamika are sitting?"

The bar maid strained to see where Jackson was talking about through the darken room Jackson took his hand and pointed to Tyrone and Tamika.

Realizing what table Jackson was talking about she quickly went to the bar to get their order.

Tamika started to feel uncomfortable as she watched Jackson and the two women he sat with laugh and drink.

Tyrone noticing Tamika`s mood change asked "What`s wrong Baby is there anything I did?"

"No your fine it`s not you" said Tamika.

Tamika not wanting to ruin the night said "After we have another drink I would like to leave if you don`t mind."

Tyrone could see the feelings she had for Jackson weren`t completely gone. Seeing Tamika`s mood change gave Tyrone an attitude.

While Tamika and Tyrone talked, the bar maid brought over the bottle of champagne Jackson had sent them.

Tyrone noticed Jackson hold up his glass and toast to them. Tyrone looking in to Tamika`s eyes said, "Lets toast to a wonderful future together."

After hearing Tyrone`s toast Tamika began to relax, because she knew she would never have a future with Jackson.

Smiling she said, "Starting tonight I`m all yours if you want me" Tyrone felt like he could conquer the world, knowing that Tamika was willing to stand by his side.

Jackson put down his glass and turned his attention once again to his two lovely dates.

Tamika drank a few glasses of champagne and said, "Tyrone are you ready to go?"

Tyrone asked, "Are you alright?"

Tamika just smiled and said, "I'm fine baby."

Tyrone rose to his feet and grabbed Tamika by the hand and led her to the table where Jackson was sitting with his two dates.

Tyrone extended his hand and told Jackson thank you for everything.

Jackson stood up and grabbed Tyrone's hand and pulled him in close to hug him then releasing Tyrone Jackson extended his hand to Tamika.

Tamika reluctantly shook Jackson's hand once their hands touched, Jackson pulled her in to his chest and hugged her in his strong arms.

While hugging her he whispered and said, "I told you it would work,"

"I know you and him will be really happy together."

Then she whispered back and said, "I know",

"We will be good for one another."

Smiling Jackson released Tamika and said, "Have a good night."

While Jackson was saying good night Tamika looked at Tyrone and knew she had made the right choice.

Feeling secure about her decision Tamika said, "Good night Jackson and thank you." Tyrone hearing Tamika thank Jackson gave him more confidence than ever.

He could see that Tamika was letting go of her feelings for Jackson and he knew she was with him one hundred percent. Tyrone grabbed Tamika's hand and they headed for the exit.

Outside Tyrone quickly put his jacket around Tamika's shoulders.

Tamika smiled and said, "I don't need it now." Tyrone asked, "Why not?"

Tamika looked at Tyrone and said, "That was when I thought I was going to have to stand in that long line."

"But after such a lovely date."

"I feel warm all over,"

"And I do mean warm all over."

They reached the car Tyrone opened Tamika's door, and walked over to the other side to get in.

 Once inside Tamika started the car and let the car warm up, as they sat there Tyrone said, "Tamika I really do like you."

"I need to be honest with you."

"I hope this doesn't change the way you feel about me,"

"But I need to be honest."

"You probably think I have money because of the clothes I have on and the shoes I'm wearing."

"But the truth is Jackson let me borrow this fly ass suit and these shoes."

"I don`t have the kind of money to afford things like this."

"I do have a job but I don`t have the things that Jackson has."

Tamika began to shish Tyrone as she put her hands softly on his lips. Tamika spoke up after she had stopped Tyrone`s confession.

"Baby all I need is you."

"If you treat me like you treated me tonight,"

"Then I`ll take care of all the rest.

Tyrone removed Tamika`s hand from his mouth and said, "Baby I would never think of taking anything from you"

"I`m not a user."

Tamika interrupted Tyrone and said, "You're not using me I`m offering."

"If you're going to be my man., then were in this together, you feel me? "

Tyrone was speechless he had never met a women like Tamika. Tamika smiled and said, "You`ve been a perfect gentleman all night."

"I felt like this was a dream come true."

"I was a little disturbed when I saw Jackson with those two women."

"But then I realized they`ll only have fun for tonight,"

"And tomorrow they`ll only have a memory."

"But when I wake up in the morning I`ll still have you,"

"Knowing that I'm more than happy with you."

Tyrone smiled and said, "I left my car at Jackson's house,"

"Do you mind taking me over there to get it?"

Tamika just smiled and said, "I'll take you tomorrow."

"It will be just fine where it's at tonight."

She began pulling out of her parking spot and headed for the expressway.

Tyrone seeing Tamika headed in the wrong direction from his house asked, "Where are you going I live the opposite way?"

Tamika laughed and said, "You're all mine tonight to do whatever I want to do,"

"Remember this is our anniversary and I'm not done celebrating."

Tyrone laughed and leaned back, Tamika had made all his dreams come true.

Chapter Fourteen

As Jackson and his dates were drinking and laughing Shirley smiled at Jackson and asked,

"Do you remember any good times when we together in high school."

Jackson said, "Baby I`ve never forgot about you."

"I remember you have a small mole on the inside of your right thigh."

"I used to love to use the tip of my tongue to play with it, do you remember that?"

Shirley began to blush and giggle.

"I see you haven`t forgot where my spot is."

Jackson held his glass up to his lips and slowly began to dip his tongue in and out of his glass as if he was dipping his tongue in and out of her pussy.

Debbie hearing Jackson and Shirley flirt said, "I feel left out."

Jackson smiled and said, "Baby don't worry there's plenty to go around."

Debbie smiled and asked Jackson, "Do you think you can handle both of us at the same time."

Jackson laughed and said, "If Tupac made it rapping then we can make it happen, you feel me"?

Now that Debbie was getting some of Jackson's attention she was ready for whatever.

Jackson seeing the bottle of champagne was almost gone stood up and said, "It's a little crowded in here."

"Do you two ladies mind if we take this party to my house?"

Shirley looked at Debbie and said, "I will if you will."

Debbie spoke up and said, "I'm all yours."

Looking at both ladies Jackson smiled. It had been a while since he had been with two women at the same time.

But he was excited seeing the willingness of both ladies. Jackson extended both his hands one to each lady and raising them to their feet they drank the last of the champagne and prepared to leave.

Now that everyone was ready, Jackson walked to the bar to take care of his tab.

Jackson reached into his pocket and handed the bar maid two hundred and fifty dollars.

The bar maid counted the money and said, "This is fifty dollars to much,"

Jackson said, "The extra fifty is your tip."

Smiling the bar maid made a mental note to try and get Jackson`s attention the next time she seen him. He smiled at the bar maid and escorted both ladies to their car.

Shirley and Debbie got in and warmed their car up.

As they were sitting there warming up their car Jackson said, "I`ll pull my car over in a minute and you two can follow me." Jackson went and got his car and pulled over to where they were waiting for him.

Shirley pulled out from the parking spot and began to follow Jackson.

Close behind Jackson Debbie spoke up and said, "Shirley I`ve never been with another woman before."

Shirley looked Debbie in her eyes and said, "We`ve been friends for a while."

"I always used to watch you and wondered what it would be like to be with you."

"Now that we have an opportunity to be with each other I promise to make it the most enjoyable time you`ll ever have."

Debbie looked and said, "I used to wonder how you tasted to."

"I sometimes masturbate and I think about being with you,"

"But I never had the nerve to tell you."

Shirley took her free hand and placed it on Debbie's thigh and began to caress her softly.

She slowly slid her hand up to her pussy and pulled her panties to the side and began trying to push her fingers inside of her.

Debbie seeing her having have difficulties trying to drive and attend to her pussy said, "Let me help you".

Debbie raised her hips slightly off the seat and raising her dress up to her stomach she pulled her panties down to her ankles and slid each leg out.

Then she leaned the seat back to expose her awaiting pussy. Debbie grabbed Shirley's hand and placed it back on her pussy and said, "Is that better"

"Now you can do whatever you want."

Shirley slid her fingers in between Debbie's plump pussy lips and began to gently rub her clitoris.

The soft touch of Shirley's fingers aroused Debbie's clitoris and made it become hard and rigid. Debbie reached inside her dress and pulled out one of her breast and started to play with her nipple.

Shirley feeling the heat from Debbie's body made her want to explore Debbie's pussy even more.

Moving past her clitoris she made her way down to her moistened pussy, she began sliding her fingers in and out. At first only one at a time then she inserted two.

Debbie's legs parted wider welcoming her fingers to go inside. Moaning she said, "Go deeper."

Shirley took her fingers and pushed them inside as far as she could. Debbie pushed her pussy onto her fingers and began to rotate her hips to push them in and out of her pussy.

Shirley seeing Jackson`s Brake lights she pulled her hand from pussy and told Debbie to put her panties back on.

Debbie smiled and said, "I can`t wait to return the favor." Placing her breast back inside her dress and putting her panties back on she sat the seat back up to its normal position. Pulling in front of Jackson`s house they looked at each other and smiled.

Jackson in his rear view mirror could see Debbie leaning back in the passenger side seat was wondering if Debbie might have passed out from the drinks.

Jackson was hoping she hadn`t gotten to drunk where she couldn`t participate.

Then he said to himself Shirley was still available so he wouldn`t be to upset.

Excited about what about to take place Jackson took the fastest way home. As Jackson pulled up to his house, he noticed that Debbie was sitting up once again.

Jackson was thinking I`m glad she was awake, now we can really have some fun.

As Shirley and Debbie parked, Jackson waited on the sidewalk for the two women to exit their car. As Shirley and Debbie exited the car Shirley began to lick her fingers.

Jackson seeing her lick her fingers was thinking she was licking them for him, not knowing what had transpired in the car between the two women.

Jackson opened the door and invited the two women inside. Inside they both sat on the couch and asked Jackson if they could have another drink?

Jackson only had a half a bottle of wine left. Strolling into the kitchen for some glasses Jackson was excited thinking what was about to happen.

Bringing the glasses back into the family room he sat down and poured them each a glass of wine.

Jackson began to toast, first pointing his glass at Shirley he said, "To old friends and to new friends" then pointing his glass at Debbie.

Finishing his toast they all drank their glass of wine. Debbie said, "I feel warm already."

Jackson just smiled, and said, "I have something special for us."

Jackson went to his secret stash and got a bottle of clear liquor.

Debbie asked "What is that"?

As Jackson held the bottle up to the women he said, "This is guaranteed to get your pussy wet"

"This is white lighting."

Debbie laughed and said, "I aint no stranger to that my daddy used to drink that all the time."

"We used to steal a nip or two from time to time."

Jackson laughed and poured everybody a shot of white lighting.

After they drank their shot of white lighting Debbie began to take off all her clothes.

Jackson said it is a little warm in here and he took off all his clothes.

Debbie and Jackson turned to Shirley and asked, "Are you going to join us"?

Shirley laughed and said "Sure" and immediately got naked.

Jackson leaned back on the couch Who do you want first?"

Jackson looked at both women and said, "I'd rather see you two go at it."

Debbie looked at Shirley and said, "We can pick up where we left off in the car."

Jackson laughed and asked Debbie "Is that why you were laid back in the car"?

Shirley laughed and said, "I didn't know you seen that".

Jackson laughed and said, "I really didn't know what was going on".

"But now that I know, now I can get a show, you feel me"?

Shirley stood up first and said, "If it's a show you want then it's a show you'll get". Shirley walked over to Debbie and parted her legs.

Sliding in between Debbie's legs she slowly began to slide her fingers inside of her. As Debbie leaned her head back on the couch.

She began to relax and completely surrendered to her passions. Standing up and taking her fingers from inside of her. Shirley bent over Debbie and began to kiss her passionately.

With Shirley`s tongue sliding in and out of her mouth, Debbie reached up and began to gently massage Shirley`s supple breast and gently squeezed her nipples.

While still massaging Shirley`s breast Debbie eased one of her hands up to Shirley`s pussy to be met by a gush of hot wetness awaiting her.

She gently slid her fingers inside to retrieve some of the tasty pussy juice and slid her hand back to her awaiting mouth and replaced Shirley`s tongue with her pussy flavored fingers.

Tasting her hot pussy juices she began to softly moan while sucking on her fingers.

With Debbie still sucking her fingers Shirley eased down to her knees and began to suck Debbie`s hard awaiting nipples. She went from one breast to the other, being was careful not to give one more attention than she gave the other.

Shirley began to slide down and kiss Debbie`s quivering stomach, slowly working her way down to her already hot wet pussy.

Shirley reached down and placed Debbie`s legs high on her shoulders and buried her head deep between her thighs.

Debbie began to moan louder and louder Jackson hearing Debbie moan made his already rock hard dick throb in his hand.

Debbie looked over at Jackson and said, "I need your hard dick in my pussy right now."

Jackson looked at Debbie and said, "Baby don`t be selfish," as he pointed to Shirley with her head still buried deep between Debbie`s thighs.

Debbie slowly eased Shirley from her pussy and raised her head to face her. Looking into her eyes Debbie took her tongue and began trying to lick every drop of pussy juice from around Shirley's mouth.

After thoroughly cleaning Shirley's face Debbie raised Shirley to her feet and reached down and grabbed her right leg and placed it across her shoulders.

Debbie then used her left hand and placed it in the small of Shirley's back to help support her. While supporting Shirley with one hand she took her free hand and parted her pussy lips exposing her throbbing clitoris.

Once Debbie had Shirley's clitoris exposed she began to gently massage it with her tongue.

Shirley feeling Debbie's tongue on her hot pussy began to cum in her mouth.

Debbie put her lips around her clitoris and began to suck and lick so softly Shirley's leg she stood on began to shake and she put her hands on Debbie's shoulders trying to push her off her pussy.

 But the suction she had created on her clitoris was like a pit bull locked on his favorite toy, she sucked as hard as she could trying to suck her pussy dry. Debbie slowly began to ease the tongue hold she had on Shirley's pussy. Jackson with a Rock hard dick stood and applauded the show they had given him.

Jackson's rock hard dick bounced up and down every time he clapped.

 Now that the two women had gotten in the mood Jackson figured it was time to put the icing on the cake. Jackson standing there with a rock hard liquored up dick couldn't decide who he wanted first.

Looking at both ladies, Jackson couldn't decide so he said, "Were going to have a dick sucking contest." Jackson turned and grabbed the bottle of white lighting and said, "Let's have another shot."

As Jackson poured the shots of liquor he began to say, "Both of you are so beautiful,"

"It's hard for me to decide who I want first,"

"I'm going to leave the decision up to you."

Debbie Laughed and said, "What's the prize?"

"Whoever can suck my dick the best will win first prize."

"It is a good fucking and a one hundred dollar grand prize."

Shirley said, "One hundred dollars, I'm in."

Shirley walked over to Jackson and pushed Jackson down on the couch then she grabbed the shot of white lighting and downed it.

Shirley got on her knees and said, "For one hundred dollars,"

"I'm going to suck the hell out of your dick".

Debbie sat down beside Jackson and watched Shirley begin to suck Jackson's dick. Shirley took Jackson's dick in her hand and laid his dick flat up against his stomach.

Then she slowly began to flicker her tongue across the shaft of his dick working her way all the way up to the head.

Then she eased her mouth around the head of his dick and began to softly suck until the head of his dick disappeared in her mouth.

Shirley eased the head of his dick in and out of her mouth teasing Jackson.

Jackson looked at Debbie playing with her pussy as Shirley attended to Jackson's dick.

Debbie was getting so turned on watching Shirley suck Jackson's dick, that she leaned over and began to suck on Jackson's nipples.

Debbie got on her knees so she could suck Jackson's nipples and still play with her pussy. Debbie began to work her way from one nipple to the other.

 Then she stood up on the couch facing Jackson and eased her way up to Jackson's mouth and began to kiss him passionately.

Once they had kissed Debbie laid Jackson's head on the back of the couch and she began to straddle his face.

Debbie reached down and took both hands spreading her pussy lips exposing a hot, wet throbbing clitoris. Then she leaned forward placing her pussy into Jackson's mouth.

 Jackson began to lick her pussy so softly. Debbie's legs began to shake and Jackson began to increase the pressure licking her pussy harder and harder. Jackson could tell Debbie was on the verge of having an orgasm.

Jackson took his middle finger and began to trust it inside of Debbie's ass hole while he sucked her hot wet pussy. Once his finger was buried in her ass up to his knuckle she began to cum.

Jackson had to lean his head back as far as he could, the amount of pussy juice that came from Debbie's pussy was stopping Jackson from breathing.

The pussy juice ran down Jackson's chin on to his chest, and down to his stomach. Shirley still sucking Jackson's dick could see the pussy juice flow down Jackson's body and it turned her on.

She slid Jackson's dick to the side and began to lap up all the pussy juice she could that flowed down Jackson's body.

Debbie was starting to feel weak from the orgasm Jackson had just caused her to have.

Tapping Jackson on the top of his head Debbie asked Jackson if he could let her down.

Jackson took his finger out of her ass hole and allowed her to ease down his body and return to the seat beside him.

Shirley on her knees still cleaning Jackson's body with her tongue looked at Debbie's legs shake asked,

"Was he better than me?"

Debbie laughed and said, "You have to see for yourself."

So Shirley stood up and climbed up Jackson's body and mounted his face and began to fuck Jackson's mouth trying to cum as her friend had cum.

Jackson asked Debbie to hand him his shot of white lighting as he ate Shirley pussy. Debbie grabbed the white lighting and handed it to Jackson.

Jackson while still licking Shirley's pussy slowly poured the shot down her stomach.

The white lighting flowed down her body on to her hot pussy into Jackson`s awaiting mouth. The taste of white lighting and pussy juice mix made Jackson start to suck extremely hard forcing Shirley`s knees to buckle.

As her knees buckled she let out a loud moan and began to cum in Jackson`s mouth.

Losing her strength from the orgasm she slid down Jackson`s body with her feet still straddling Jackson`s Body.

Once her knees had given out she sat down, not realizing her wet pussy was aiming for Jackson`s throbbing hard dick.

Once Jackson`s dick touched her wet pussy, it slid inside Shirley`s hot pussy and she had an immediate orgasm.

Her pussy began to pulsate squirting cum down Jackson`s dick Jackson began to laugh and said, "You cheated."

Shirley still sitting on Jackson`s dick said, "How did I cheat." Jackson looked Shirley in her eyes and said, "You didn`t give Debbie a chance to win the prize."

"You just sat on my dick and came all over it,"

"Debbie didn`t get a chance to try to win the prize."

Shirley eased Jackson`s rock hard dick from inside of her and said, "I`m sorry Debbie,"

"I didn`t mean to be so selfish I was just caught up in the moment."

Debbie smiled and said, "It`s alright,"

"Now his dick is flavored with all that good pussy juice."

Debbie got on her knees and began sucking Jackson's dick enjoying the taste of Shirley juices that covered it.

As Shirley sat down beside Jackson, Jackson asked, "Shirley please pour us another shot of white lighting."

Shirley poured them a shot and Jackson and Shirley drank their shot of white lighting while Debbie still sucked the pussy juice from Jackson's dick.

Jackson said, "I think I've had too much to drink because I can't tell who won" Jackson eased Debbie's mouth off his dick and said, "I think It's a tie,"

"You two can split the prize."

Jackson reached over and handed Debbie her shot of white lighting and said, "We would of had waited

For you but you were a little busy." Debbie started to laugh.

Debbie stopped laughing and downed her shot then Jackson stood her on her feet and said, "I want you ride my dick like you've never rode a dick before."

Debbie smiled and started to straddle Jackson's Dick. She placed her feet flat on the couch and lowered her hot pussy on to Jackson's dick.

She took her hands and placed them under Jackson's arms to give herself a sturdy hold then she began to rock up and down on Jackson's dick.

Once Jackson's entire dick was inside of her she buried her head in Jackson's chest, and began to pinch Jackson's nipples with her teeth.

While Debbie rode Jackson Shirley got down on her knees and began to lick Jackson`s balls.

Seeing Debbie`s pussy making Jackson`s dick disappear, Shirley paused from attending to Jackson`s balls and she slid her tongue up and awaited for Debbie to descend down Jackson`s dick.

Once she had engulfed Jackson`s entire dick with her hot wet pussy. Shirley reached up placing her hands around Debbie`s hips and stopped Debbie from raising up

Holding Debbie firmly in place on Jackson`s dick she began to trust her tongue in to Debbie awaiting ass hole.

Debbie began to dig her nails in to Jackson`s shoulders and she arched her back allowing Shirley full access to her ass.

Shirley seeing Debbie arch her back took her tongue out of Debbie`s ass and licked her fingers and slowly inserted them in to her ass.

Debbie began to trust back and forth fucking Jackson`s dick as well as receiving Shirley`s fingers in her ass.

Jackson could feel the heat building inside of Debbie`s pussy and she began to squeeze Jackson`s dick hard with her hot wet pussy.

Jackson raised Debbie`s head from his chest and he began to force his tongue deep into her throat.

As they kissed Debbie could taste the pussy from his lips.

The sweet taste of pussy in her mouth and rock hard dick inside her and the fingers in her ass took her to a place she had never experienced before.

Debbie closed her eyes and allowed the pleasure to will her body and then it happened. She had the best orgasm she had ever experienced before.

All of her muscles in her whole body tightened and began to tingle all over waking up every nerve in her body causing an indescribable pleasure to overtake her senses. Feeling exhilarated and overwhelmed at the same time she nearly passed out. Debbie loosened her grip on Jackson and rolled off his dick completely exhausted once laying there she drifted off into a deep slumber.

As she lay beside Jackson in a fetal position sleeping Jackson felt proud, smiling he said", Dam I`m good."

Shirley still feeling like she hadn't had enough climbed on to Jackson's dick and began to ride it trying to make herself cum.

Shirley sat straight up on Jackson`s dick and reached down and began to violently pinch Jackson`s nipples.

Shirley began to ride Jackson`s dick so hard Jackson could feel her pelvic bone grinding in to his hips.

Jackson decided he had enough and closed his eyes to concentrate on Cumming.

Shirley arched her back as she rode Jackson`s dick hard and she began to squeeze his dick with her pussy making it feel like a hand was massaging his dick inside her, trying to coax the cum from his dick.

Jackson opened his eyes and exploded deep inside Shirley pussy. Shirley realizing Jackson had cum unsaddled his dick and said, "I wasn`t finished yet."

Jackson looked at Shirley and said, "Give me a few minutes and I`ll see what I can do for you."

With Jackson exhausted and Debbie sleep Shirley got an attitude, she put on her clothes and headed for the door, not thinking to wake up Debbie to take her with her.

Jackson still half-conscious couldn't object to Shirley leaving her friend there and could only watch as she exited the front door.

Feeling over whelmed by all the alcohol he had consumed and the physically demanding sex they had he slowly closed his eyes and drifted off into unconsciousness. After his brief rest and still feeling a little drunk he awoke Debbie and asked her if she was ready to go.

Finding his pants Jackson reached in to his pocket and handed Debbie the prize money of one hundred dollars.

Debbie said, "Thank you Jackson but the money isn't necessary." Jackson said, "Baby, a night like this is priceless so this money is only a small token of my appreciation."

Debbie smiled and took the money and put it in her purse.

As she got dressed she asked Jackson if she could do one more thing for him.

Debbie told Jackson she always had a fantasy of putting on some red lipstick and sucking someone's dick.

Jackson looked and said, "Sure if that's what you want to do," "But it's not necessary."

Debbie reached into her purse and retrieved the tube of ruby red Mac lipstick and she got on her knees and smeared the lipstick real heavy across her lips and began to suck Jackson's dick smearing the lipstick all the way down Jackson's dick. Jackson lay back trying to enjoy the pleasure she was giving him. But the liquor and the exhaustion wasn't allowing Jackson to enjoy the service he was receiving.

Jackson put his hands on her shoulders and asked her to stop. Jackson said, "Thank you but I think I need to get some sleep."

"Debbie I've had a wonderful evening," "But I'm going to call you a cab and call it a night."

Debbie smiled and said, "I do understand she stood up and walked over to the phone and called a cab." Jackson sat on the couch feeling like he had been beaten up.

Debbie sat down beside Jackson and waited for her cab to arrive. The sound of a car pulling into Jackson's drive came in to the house.

Hearing the cab outside, Jackson stood up put on his trousers and kissed Debbie good night and let her out.

Once he had locked the door Jackson said, "What a day it's been,"

"I will never forget October the 27th."

As he climbed the steps, he could feel the effect of all the liquor and wine he had consumed. Jackson went to his bedroom, laid in the bed and took a deep breath, feeling over whelmed he closed his eyes and gave in to the tiredness that over took him.

THE END

www.ingramcontent.com/pod-product-compliance
Lightning Source LLC
Chambersburg PA
CBHW020245150626
46552CB00020B/415